"If all I wanted was to keep my land, I could have married anyone,"

Jonas told her.

Colleen went very still. "What are you trying to say?"

He couldn't go back now—and he didn't want to. "It wasn't the idea of saving my land that kept drawing me to you, Colleen."

"I don't believe that."

"Then believe this," he murmured, lowering his head to hers.

Colleen's gasp was instantly stifled by his mouth, and her surprise was quickly replaced by desire. She'd tried for so long to fight her growing feelings for him, but she wanted this; she wanted him.

His mouth tore away from hers, then slid along her throat, tasting the sweetness of her skin.

"Jonas—" her voice was a broken whisper "—don't hurt me."

Wanting desperately to reassure her, he buried his hands in her hair and cradled her head. "I could never hurt you, Colleen. I want to love you—like this—forever."

Dear Reader:

Happy October! The temperature is crisp, the leaves on the trees are putting on their annual color show and the daylight hours are getting shorter. What better time to cuddle up with a good book? What better time for Silhouette Romance?

And in October, we've got an extraspecial lineup. Continuing our DIAMOND JUBILEE celebration is Stella Bagwell—with *Gentle as a Lamb*. The wolf is at shepherdess Colleen McNair's door until she meets up with Jonas Dobbs—but is he friend or the ultimate foe? Only by trusting her heart can she tell for sure.... Don't miss this wonderful tale of love.

The DIAMOND JUBILEE—Silhouette Romance's tenth anniversary celebration—is our way of saying thanks to you, our readers. To symbolize the timelessness of love, as well as the modern gift of the tenth anniversary, we're presenting readers with a DIAMOND JUBILEE Silhouette Romance each month, penned by one of your favorite Silhouette Romance authors. In the coming months, writers such as Lucy Gordon and Phyllis Halldorson are writing DIAMOND JUBILEE titles especially for you.

And that's not all! There are six books a month from Silhouette Romance—stories by wonderful writers who time and time again bring home the magic of love. During our anniversary year, each book is special and written with romance in mind. October brings you *Joey's Father* by Elizabeth August—a heartwarming story with a few surprises in store for the lovely heroine and rugged hero—as well as *Make-believe Marriage*—Carole Buck's debut story in the Silhouette Romance line. *Cimarron Rebel* by Pepper Adams, the third book in the exciting CIMARRON STORIES trilogy, is also coming your way this month! And in the future, work by such loved writers as Diana Palmer, Annette Broadrick and Brittany Young is sure to put a smile on your lips.

During our tenth anniversary, the spirit of celebration is with us year-round. And that's all due to you, our readers. With the support you've given to us, you can look forward to many more years of heartwarming, poignant love stories.

I hope you'll enjoy this book and all of the stories to come. Come home to romance—Silhouette Romance—for always!

Sincerely,

Tara Hughes Gavin
Senior Editor

STELLA BAGWELL

Gentle as a Lamb

Published by Silhouette Books New York
America's Publisher of Contemporary Romance

For my husband, Harrell,
who asked for this book.
And for all our memorable trips to Colorado.
Thanks, darling.

SILHOUETTE BOOKS
300 E. 42nd St., New York, N.Y. 10017

ISBN: 0-373-08748-9

First Silhouette Books printing October 1990

Printed in the U.S.A.

Books by Stella Bagwell

Silhouette Romance

Golden Glory #469
Moonlight Bandit #485
A Mist on the Mountain #510
Madeline's Song #543
The Outsider #560
The New Kid in Town #587
Cactus Rose #621
Hillbilly Heart #634
Teach Me #657
The White Night #674
No Horsing Around #699
That Southern Touch #723
Gentle as a Lamb #748

STELLA BAGWELL

lives with her husband and teenage son in southeastern Oklahoma, where she says the weather is extreme and the people are friendly. When she isn't writing romances, she enjoys horse racing and touring the countryside on a motorcycle.

Stella is very proud to know that she can give joy to others through her books. And now, thanks to the Oklahoma Library for the Blind in Oklahoma City, she is able to reach an even bigger audience. The library has transcribed her novels onto cassette tapes so that blind people across the state can also enjoy them.

A Note From The Author:

Dear Reader,

Since Silhouette Romance began ten years ago, it's been a part of my life—first as a reader, then later as a writer. So it is a special privilege for me to be a part of the DIAMOND JUBILEE celebration.

In November 1985, I sold my first Silhouette Romance. Now, thirteen books later, it is still a thrill to see each new one in print. Creating stories of two people meeting and ultimately finding love and happiness is a job that gives me great pleasure indeed. In this fast-paced world, I believe that from time to time we all need a lift in spirit. With each book I write, I like to think I'm giving you, the reader, a good feeling in your heart, one that tells you that you are a special person.

To me, love is the thing that makes everything worthwhile, and gives us the strength to overcome the troubles life sometimes deals us. Writing romance gives me the opportunity to, hopefully, put a little love in each and every one of your lives.

I want to express my deepest thanks to all of my faithful readers, and I hope that my stories have given you as much joy as I have gotten from writing them.

God bless you all.

Love,

Stella Bagwell

Chapter One

The car was gray and obviously expensive. With cool green eyes, Colleen McNair watched it slowly pull off to the side of the narrow highway.

It was not uncommon to see cars passing on this particular highway even though it was located in a remote area in the mountains. The highway was kept in good condition, since it was the only one leading into Lake City from the north.

During the summer, tourists often made the drive from Gunnison to Lake City, and even farther down to South Fork. The towering Rocky Mountains made an awesome sight, and people were constantly stopping to look out with their cameras or binoculars at the majestic view, or simply to scan the lower slopes for wild animals. Even Colleen's sheep had received plenty of attention before. So she expected the gray car belonged to a tourist.

The early morning sun had not yet risen over the jagged peaks of the mountains, leaving Colleen's camp still shaded and chilly. It was late June, but even so, June in the Colorado mountains could be cold.

She'd already built up the campfire, cooked her breakfast, and was starting on her second cup of coffee. She sipped it slowly as she watched the door on the driver's side of the car open.

A tall man dressed in a suit and western hat climbed out, but since Colleen was camped nearly three hundred yards up and away from the highway, it was difficult to tell more than that about him. Besides, she wasn't really that curious.

Colleen lowered the cup to her lap as she realized the man had started hiking up the side of the mountain straight toward her camp. She rarely had visitors, and certainly not visitors in expensive cars.

It took Jonas about three minutes to climb the grassy slope. Dew still covered the ground and the air was crisp against his face. He'd always loved the mountains, but these days he rarely had time to enjoy them. Even this trip was business of sorts. A business he definitely wasn't looking forward to.

The woman sitting by the fire was not the Colleen McNair he remembered: a long-legged teenager with strawberry-blond hair hanging to the middle of her back, a fresh face sprinkled with freckles and a shy smile. The woman before him bore only a superficial resemblance to that girl, but then it had been at least ten years since he'd seen her.

"Hello," he said, once he was close enough to be heard.

"Hello," she replied.

Her voice was cool and husky. She'd obviously been sizing him up from the moment he'd started up the mountain.

"Can I help you?" she went on. "If you're worried about being lost—"

He shook his head. "No, I'm not lost. I'm—" He was only a few feet away from her now. He met her curious gaze and decided her sober expression needed to be greeted with a smile. "I don't suppose you remember me, do you?"

She looked at him for a long moment, and then something flared in her eyes. "You're Jonas Dobbs."

Her voice was flat now, as was the expression on her face. Jonas didn't let it put him off. In his line of work he was used to negative reactions.

"I didn't know if you'd remember me."

"I do."

"I believe the last time I saw you was at Roger's wedding. You had on a straw hat with a green ribbon."

Colleen was surprised he'd noticed her, much less remembered what she'd worn. He was in her cousin Roger's social circle, whereas Colleen didn't fit in a circle of any sort.

"And what brings you all the way out here, Mr. Dobbs? Surely not to discuss a wedding that took place over ten years ago."

He smiled faintly, and in spite of herself Colleen realized Jonas Dobbs had matured into a handsome man. He had dark skin and hair and gray eyes. His nose was too large, but it went well with the rest of his face, which was strong and craggy, and very masculine.

His body was tall and thickset, with heavy muscles that weren't quite disguised by the lightweight material of his slacks and jacket. She remembered him wearing jeans and western shirts. But now that Jonas Dobbs was a lawyer, he'd probably put that sort of clothes aside, she thought.

He cleared his throat and stepped closer to the ring of rocks encircling the small fire. "Actually I'm here because of Roger. We've kept in touch through the years, even after he left Gunnison and moved back to Kansas. He's very concerned about you, Miss McNair."

A short, harsh laugh burst from Colleen. It was the only response she made.

Jonas grimaced, then went on. "He knows your father has been dead for over six months now. You're living up here in the mountains alone, and—"

"Roger doesn't care about that! He's more worried about getting his hands on the land my father left me."

"Miss McNair, I think you're mistaken—"

"No, it's you who are mistaken, Mr. Dobbs," she said dryly, suddenly feeling very defensive. "And if you're up here acting as his lawyer, then you've made an even bigger mistake."

Jonas looked around for a place to sit, but found none.

Colleen said, "Sorry, I don't have any more camp chairs. I'm not usually overrun by visitors."

"That's all right," he assured her while hitching up his slacks and squatting down on his bootheels.

He had on nice black cowboy boots, Colleen noticed, that went well with his gray slacks. She was certain the boots were made of elephant hide, making them not only good to look at, but also tough and durable. She wondered if Jonas Dobbs matched his boots.

"Frankly," he said, "I wasn't aware that you and Roger were at odds with each other."

Colleen felt the urge to laugh at the gross understatement. "Roger and I have always just been cousins, not friends like the two of you."

For some inexplicable reason Jonas felt an uncomfortable warmth creep up his neck. "Do you mean Roger or his parents weren't around when your father was ill?"

Colleen shook her head. "I was around, Mr. Dobbs. Just me. A friend or two from Lake City and a few from Gunnison. They helped during his illness and—and with the funeral. Family can't be bothered about those things," she said, her voice tinged with bitterness. "Or at least the people who called themselves Dad's family couldn't be bothered."

Jonas drew in a deep breath and let it out slowly. He'd come out here to see Colleen McNair as a favor to Roger. But now he wished he hadn't committed himself. Especially when he looked into Colleen McNair's shadowed green eyes.

"I'm sorry," he said.

She studied him from beneath long golden lashes. There was something about his face and his voice that almost made her believe him.

"How do you manage out here alone? Sheep herding is—"

"A lowly life," she finished for him.

He took off his hat and Colleen watched his large hand tunnel through the dark waves on his head. He had strong-looking hands. She wondered if he ever used them for anything physical or if they merely worked at pushing a pencil and telephone buttons.

"I was going to say a lonely life," he said.

She looked away from him and tossed the dregs of her coffee into the fire.

"It is. At times. But it's my life," she said.

He let his eyes travel around the camp, taking in the small brown tent, the open fire and the blackened cooking pots sitting to one side, and finally the sheepdog lying asleep at Colleen's feet. About a thousand yards up the mountain was a large flock of Hampshire sheep. The tinkling of the bells around their necks carried in the light mountain air. Every now and then the tinkling was joined by bleats and baas. Somewhere in the distance he could hear a mountain stream rushing and tumbling toward Lake Fork creek.

Jonas couldn't imagine anyone living so solitarily, especially a young woman who, if given the proper chance, could be beautiful.

At the moment she was wearing a pair of faded jeans, hiking boots and a thick gray sweatshirt. Her hair, which he'd remembered as being long and shiny was now cropped close to her head with straight bangs across her forehead. She was very slender, making the lines of her face sharp and angular. She reminded him of a starving kitten that couldn't quite make up its mind on whether to hiss and claw to protect itself, or mew for help.

"How long do you stay out here at a time?" he asked.

She absently rubbed her hands down the thighs of her jeans and Jonas noticed that even though her hands were slender and fine-boned they still looked like work hands with their blunt nails and rough skin.

"About six weeks or so. Until the grass is gone. I drive back to the house at times and leave Dangit with the sheep. He watches them as well as I do."

The collie dog at her feet raised his head and whined at the mention of his name. "You take care of them for me. Don't you, boy?" she asked the dog as she stroked his head.

"Roger seems to think you'd be better off living in Gunnison, doing clerical work or something of that sort. What do you think, Miss McNair?"

She met his eyes and smiled faintly. "I think Roger is a pompous ass."

His thick dark brows lifted. "And me?"

One of Colleen's shoulders rose and fell. "I don't believe you really know Roger. Otherwise, you wouldn't have bothered driving all the way out here."

He had to concede that was true. And even though this wasn't a life he thought suited for a woman, he could see that Colleen McNair had been taking care of herself for a long time.

"Well, I'd better be getting back to town," he said, rising back up to his full height. He extended his hand out to her. "It was nice seeing you again, Miss McNair. Take care of yourself."

She took his offered hand and for a moment his strong warm fingers curled around hers. It had been a long time since she'd had any physical contact with another person, particularly a man. She was keenly aware of Jonas Dobbs as he stepped away from her.

"I will, Mr. Dobbs. Goodbye."

She watched him walk back down to his car. As he got in and drove off, she realized she had yet to move from her seat, and if her mother were still alive she'd be shaming her unmercifully for not offering her visitor a cup of coffee.

Well, it was too late to be worrying about manners now, she thought. Besides, Jonas Dobbs probably believed she didn't know anything about manners anyway.

"Come on, Dangit, let's go check on the lambs," she told the dog.

The two of them started up the mountain between a stand of Colorado blue spruce. Below them, Jonas Dobbs turned his car around and headed back to Gunnison.

Jonas's law office was located on the west end of town. It was nearly lunch when he pulled his car into a space at the back of the brick building.

Once inside his office he tossed his hat on a rack on the wall, then sat down in the rich leather chair behind his desk. "Opal, I'm back," he said after buzzing his secretary on the intercom. "If you'd like to go on to lunch now, that's fine with me."

"Thank you, Jonas. I'll take a short one."

"No need to hurry, Opal," he assured the older woman. "I have a few phone calls to make anyway."

"Okay, Jonas. Would you like for me to bring you back a sandwich?"

He thought for a moment and decided he wasn't really hungry. "No, thanks, Opal. I'll have something later."

After flipping through his rolodex, Jonas punched out a number. He leaned back in the chair and propped his boots on the edge of the desk.

"Roger Boyd, please," he spoke to the female voice on the end of the line.

"May I ask who's calling?"

The corners of Jonas's mouth lifted wryly. "Just tell him it's Jonas."

Moments later a masculine voice sounded in his ear. "Jonas, old boy, good to hear from you. How are things out in Colorado?"

"Things are fine with me, Roger."

"I take it you're calling to tell me you've been out to see Colleen?"

Instead of seeing the paneled walls of his law office, Jonas was suddenly picturing Colleen McNair on the side of the mountain, her sad green eyes, her work-roughened hands.

"That's right."

"And? Did you convince her she needs to sell?"

"I didn't mention it to her," Jonas said smoothly.

"Didn't mention it!" Roger blurted. "Jonas, I thought our discussion earlier was to—"

"Look, Roger," Jonas cut in, "Colleen is doing what she wants to do. It was obvious to me from the moment I saw her that she has no desire at all to sell her land. She's been through enough over losing her father without badgering the woman about her home."

"For God's sake, I didn't want you to badger her, Jonas! You've always been a charmer. If anyone can talk any sense into that spinster it would be you."

His face tight, Jonas pulled his boots down from the desk. "Roger, we've been friends for a long time. But if I ever hear you say anything like that again, it's going to be the end of things."

"Oh, now Jonas," Roger said, his voice suddenly patronizing. "You know exactly what I mean. You always were diplomatic. Women listen to you. All I wanted you to do was talk common sense to her. She doesn't need to be living out there alone, doing a man's job. Don't you agree?"

"I see your reasoning," he said. But Colleen's words had cast a seed of doubt in his mind about Roger's motivation.

"It would be much easier for her to live in town. Good Lord, no normal woman would ever dream of living the way she does."

"So you're saying Colleen is strange for choosing how she wants to live?"

Roger sputtered with disbelief at Jonas's statement. "I damn well know she's strange! Don't you remember her? She was so shy and backward her face would turn beet-red if you said two words to her. She and her daddy lived like hermits back in those mountains. Damned if I know how she ever—" Roger suddenly broke off.

Jonas prodded curiously, "How she ever what?"

"Nothing," he said quickly. "So what did Colleen have to say?"

Jonas frowned. "She seems to think you want her land."

"I do. That's no secret."

"But why do you want it, Roger?"

The line went silent for a few tense moments. Finally Roger asked, "What did she do? Paint me as the evil cousin who's trying to steal it?"

Jonas's nostrils flared with indignation. "I guess you've forgotten I'm a lawyer. I'm capable of drawing my own conclusions."

"Hmm. Sounds like she really did a number on you, buddy."

Jonas's jaws clamped down tightly, making his teeth grind together. Colleen had said he hadn't really known Roger. Maybe she was right. "No one does a number on me, Roger. Not even you. I talked to your cousin. She's happy where she is. My advice is to leave it. You're in Kansas now, anyway. Purchase land there."

Roger made a frustrated sound. "Jonas, Colleen lives a rough life in those mountains. I'm just trying to give her a chance at something better. My Lord, she's out there all alone; anything could happen to her. It's not a place I'd want for my wife or daughter to be. Neither would you."

Letting out a long breath, Jonas rubbed his fingers across his forehead. Some of what Roger said made sense. Still, a person had the right to choose where and how they wanted to live.

"No, I wouldn't but—"

"Look, Jonas, Colleen is just looking at things sentimentally, not realistically. You need to make her see this."

"Maybe you should fly out here and make her see it yourself," Jonas retorted. "After all, she is your family."

"That's exactly why I can't. She views me as an interfering relative. Hopefully she'll view you as an objective outsider."

Closing his eyes, Jonas wished he'd never gotten himself involved in any of this. "She sees me as your friend, which, frankly, ruins my reputation in Colleen's opinion. And in my own opinion I'd be crazy to have anything else to do with this."

Roger's chuckle was confident, as though he considered Jonas's reluctance as merely temporary. "Aw, Jonas, you know you don't mean that. You've always had a compassionate streak in you. I know you'd like to see Colleen do herself better just as much as I would."

Jonas absently tapped a pen against his calendar book. "Maybe so. But it's not my business to butt into hers. Besides, after seeing her today, I don't think hell or high water would move her off that land," Jonas told him.

There was a slight pause, then Roger said, "I think it's going to be much easier than you think, Jonas."

Jonas tossed the pen aside and planted his elbows on the desktop. "What do you mean?"

"Well, I just mean that her father left Colleen in a hell of a financial mess. She needs money, otherwise she's not going to have any land, period."

This was news to Jonas and suddenly he saw things in a totally different light. Colleen McNair wasn't just a woman alone. She was also a woman in need. And he knew exactly how she was feeling. Because in a way he was backed against the wall, too.

"I'll try again, Roger. That's about all I can promise."

"Great, Jonas! I knew I could count on you."

The two men went on to exchange a few more words before they said their goodbyes. Jonas's expression was grim when he finally hung up the telephone. He didn't like being used by a friend, which was exactly what Roger was doing. He should have told him flat-out that he would have nothing to do with Colleen or her land. But each time he'd started to speak the words, Colleen's face, so wistful and so determined, had drifted through his mind. It was a face he could not forget, and he wondered a bit ominously if he'd stepped into something that he'd eventually regret, in more ways than one.

Three days later, Colleen was back at her farmhouse doing the laundry she'd dirtied out at the sheep camp. While she waited for the last load on the clothesline to dry, she went to the kitchen to make a few sandwiches to take with her.

It was early evening and she was anxious to be on her way. Once the sun fell behind the mountains it quickly became dark, and she wanted to be back with Dangit and the sheep before then. Besides, she didn't enjoy being at the farmhouse anymore. It held too many unpleasant memories for her. Especially her father's bedroom, where he'd lain ill and bedridden with cancer for several months.

Out on the mountain she could put the memory of his frail, pain-racked body out of her mind, or at least to the back of her mind where it didn't hurt quite so much.

Since Dangit was with the sheep, there was no bark to warn her that someone had pulled up outside the house. When a knock sounded at the front door, she jumped at the unexpected noise.

Guesses as to who the caller might be ran through her mind as she wiped her hands on a dish towel and headed to the front of the house.

To Colleen's utter amazement, Jonas Dobbs stood on the steps. This time he was wearing jeans and a plaid western shirt of a deep burgundy color. He held his cream-colored hat between his big hands.

Colleen stood there looking at him, her surprise giving way to wariness. There was only one reason why Jonas Dobbs would take the time to drive back to see her. Her cousin was at it again.

"I hope I'm not intruding," he said.

Colleen blushed as she realized she had yet to say anything. "I was just getting ready to leave," she said truthfully.

"This won't take long. I promise," he assured her.

He could see the indecision in her eyes. Jonas realized it bothered him to have her think he was the enemy. Which was rather strange for him. In his line of work he was often viewed as the enemy and it had never bothered him in the least.

Colleen stepped aside and allowed him to enter the house. The living room was clean and tidy, but dusty from not being used. Colleen had few visitors at her home. The ones who did visit were her closest friends and they always went to the kitchen to relax and talk. But Jonas Dobbs was obviously not a kitchen person, so she motioned for him to take a seat on the couch.

There was a Navajo blanket spread across the back of it. As he made himself comfortable, Jonas rubbed his fingers across the nubby texture.

Colleen took a stuffed armchair across from him.

Leaning forward, she rested her elbows on her knees. "You're the last person I expected to see. I suppose I can credit Roger for this visit? Right?"

A grimace marred his features. "Not in the way you think."

She reached up and ran her fingers through the short hair across her forehead. His presence made her very nervous. Not just because he was a man, but because he represented a threat to the only life she knew. If Roger had hired Jonas Dobbs as his lawyer, she knew she would be facing a formidable opponent.

Jonas allowed his eyes to run over her. She was fragile-looking even though he knew she worked hard physically. Her complexion was tanned to a golden hue from the summer sun. Today she had on a blue short-sleeved shirt that exposed most of her arms. They were slender arms, covered with pale freckles, as was her face. There was nothing glamorous about her by any means, but there was something very feminine that struck him each time he looked at her.

"I'm not working for him in any capacity. Roger and I had a talk the other day and I decided to take it upon myself to let you know about it. I felt you needed to be warned."

Colleen's smile was mocking. "Warned? No one has to warn me about Roger. I'm aware that Roger lacks scruples."

Jonas let out a long breath. He didn't know why he'd been compelled to bother himself about this woman. He usually wasn't the knight-in-shining-armor type. But for the past three days Colleen McNair had rarely left his thoughts. "I don't know about that. I do know, however, that he's expressed his misgivings about you living out here alone. Frankly, he says you're in financial trouble and that if you don't sell the land, you're going to lose it anyway."

An uneasy chill ran down Colleen's spine. "That's none of his business."

"I agree."

She slanted him a long look beneath her lashes. "If you agree, then why are you here?"

"Because if what he says is true, I thought you might need advice, assistance."

"From you?"

"I am a lawyer," he pointed out. Jonas saw her slender shoulders suddenly sag, her hands reach up and tiredly rub her eyes. Something deep inside him stirred. He wanted to touch her, tell her she wasn't completely alone in the world. It was a crazy notion. He barely knew her.

"It was always Roger's policy to stick his nose into other people's business. It looks like nothing has changed with him."

She'd been talking more to herself than she had been to Jonas, but suddenly she stopped and looked at him. There was a hard glint in her eyes, and he decided that she and Roger had fallen out with each other long ago. But Jonas wasn't going to ask her about it. It was none of his business.

Actually Colleen's financial problems had been none of his business, either. But Jonas kept telling himself he'd always been a man of fairness, and he knew Colleen McNair had worked hard all of her life. He didn't want to see her lose her land any more than he wanted to see his own ranch taken away from him. It was a possibility that he had shoved to the back of his mind—until this year, until he'd met Colleen. Perhaps, he mused, it was time for him to face things, just as Colleen was facing them.

"Why are you here, really?" she asked. "You may not be working for Roger, but I'm sure you came out here on his behalf."

"I want to think I came out here on both your behalfs." He and Roger had been friends back in their college days at Western State. Roger had been a big socializer, the life of the party. It hadn't taken Jonas long to figure out the only reason Roger had left Kansas to go to college in Colorado was so he'd be near the ski slopes. But Jonas hadn't criticized him for that. He'd been a likable guy and, after all, most students enjoyed a little play along with their studies.

Colleen's frown was mocking. "You're Roger's friend, not mine."

"You were very young when Roger and I used to come out and hike the mountain trails." The words just came out of him. He didn't know why. Those few times he'd seen Colleen had nothing to do with now.

Her smile was a bit twisted. "Yes. You and Roger looked at me as if I were some wild little creature that belonged out on the mountains with the deer and the sheep."

"I didn't think that," he countered. In fact, he'd thought she was a little beauty, but one with a sad, lonely face. He'd even mentioned Colleen to his mother because he'd been struck by her isolated life.

Colleen laughed softly, and once again Jonas felt a strange stirring deep inside him.

"Well, you should have," she said, "because it's true. I do belong out there on the mountains. That's why I'll never let Roger or anyone take my land."

"The mortgages—"

"I'll pay them somehow," she cut in.

He sighed. "I don't want to pry, Colleen, but do you—do you have something worked out to pay them?"

He said her name so easily, as if he'd said it all her life. The sound of it coming from Jonas Dobbs surprised her much more than his question.

"Well, not exactly. But I'll do something. I've got an old pickup to sell. If necessary I'll sell some of the sheep, too."

"You can't make money without your sheep," he reasoned. "Perhaps you could get a loan."

Colleen shook her head. "Mr. Dobbs, you know how it is these days for farmers and ranchers. We're a bad risk. There isn't a bank in Colorado that would loan a woman like me money on a small herd of sheep."

He admired her for facing the reality of the situation without falling to pieces. Being from a family that had never known financial problems, he didn't know if he would be able to view things with her optimism if faced with the same situation.

"What about other relatives?" he questioned.

Colleen shook her head. "They're very distant and live in California. I have no close relatives to speak of besides Roger's mother and father."

Jonas frowned. It was unlikely she would get any help there. "I know it probably seems strange to you that I'm here, to tell you about Roger and that he knows about the mortgages. But I happen to agree with him where your welfare is concerned. Neither one of us wants to see you out here alone and struggling when you could be comfortable in—"

Colleen rolled her eyes. "Is that the line he keeps feeding you?"

"You still don't think he's sincere?" Jonas asked.

Unconsciously she rubbed her hands up and down her thighs. "You're a lawyer. I thought lawyers were trained to judge people's ulterior motives."

Jonas leaned forward and rested his forearms across his knees. "What kind of ulterior motives are we talking about?"

Colleen shrugged. "I don't know exactly. But I can tell you one thing, Mr. Dobbs. Roger wouldn't buy a piece of land just to help me out. He has a specific reason." Her eyes narrowed on Jonas's face. "Maybe you even know what it is. After all, your land runs adjacent to mine. For all I know you two could be planning on some kind of joint venture."

Shaking his head, Jonas chuckled softly. "You're a suspicious woman, aren't you?"

She eyed him soberly. "Life has taught me to be."

The smile disappeared from his face. "Yes, I suppose it has." In truth, it had taught him the same thing, and he could understand Colleen McNair's wariness. "But I promise you that if Roger has an ulterior motive, I know nothing of it. I haven't seen the man in at least two years."

Colleen let out a long breath. "Well, that's all beside the point anyway, because I have no intention of selling or losing my land."

Picking up his hat, Jonas got to his feet. There wasn't much else he could say and he didn't want to detain her any longer. He'd tried to advise her. Why did he feel he needed to do more?

Smiling, he said, "I can't fault you for that. If Roger calls again, I'll tell him no deal."

He started toward the door and once again Colleen realized she'd failed to offer him refreshment. "You'd probably like something cool to drink before your long drive back. I have iced tea in the kitchen."

"I'm sure you're busy. I wouldn't want to take up your time," he said.

Colleen rose to her feet. "It wouldn't be a bother," she told him, realizing with a shock that she wanted him to stay a few more minutes. Which didn't really make sense, she decided. Not when his presence unsettled her the way it did.

"In that case, I'd like a glass," he said, more than surprised by her offer.

She smiled tentatively at him. "If you don't mind coming to the kitchen, it's much cooler there."

"My favorite room of any house," he assured her.

Colleen led the way through the large, rambling old farmhouse. He could imagine how cold and drafty it was in the wintertime, which was at least eight months out of the year in the Colorado Rockies.

The kitchen was large. Although it had been modernized, apparently it had been done so years ago. There wasn't a microwave oven, a dishwasher or any other item of convenience that was in Jonas's own kitchen.

He took a seat at a wooden table by a row of open windows. A slight breeze fluttered the yellow curtains, and he glanced beyond them to the mountain hovering in the distance. Sunlight streamed down on the green rocky crevasses, giving the mountains a golden hue. Nearer to the house was a big tin barn. To one side of it was a stack of hay bales covered with a sheet of black plastic. He wondered how the hay got there. Did she haul it and stack it herself? Was she ever able to hire help? From the look of things, he doubted it.

The whole idea left him feeling angry at Wilton McNair. Why hadn't he urged his daughter to find a better life for herself before he'd died? Hadn't he realized how hard it would be for her once he passed on?

"Do you take sugar?"

Her husky voice interrupted his thoughts. Jonas turned away from the window to see her filling a tall glass with ice.

"No, I take it plain."

Once Colleen had the glasses filled, she carried them to the table and took a seat on the opposite end from Jonas. He was the first man who'd been in her house since her father's death, other than old Doobie. And Jonas Dobbs was nothing like old Doobie, who was at least seventy and thought of himself as a prospector.

"Thank you, this is very nice," he said, lifting the glass to his lips.

"I was just making myself some sandwiches to take back to camp. You're welcome to one."

Shaking his head, he looked at her with surprise. "You're going to your camp now? You really shouldn't drive that road after dark."

Colleen shrugged, unsure of how to take his words. She couldn't imagine him being concerned for her safety. "I know it like the back of my hand."

"It's Saturday. Some young man should be coming to take you to dinner," he said.

An odd look passed over her face.

"Sheep are my interest, not young men," she said, her voice curt. Involuntarily her eyes slipped to his left hand. There was no wedding band, and she tried to remember if she'd ever heard of him marrying. Surely the man was married, she reasoned. He was good-looking and affluent, definitely not a man to be ignored by the opposite sex.

"When do you ever get away? You have to come into town sometime," he asked.

Colleen sipped her tea. "I do. When it's necessary."

"Do you only do things when they're necessary?"

She'd never thought of it that way, but she supposed that was what she did do. "I don't have the time or luxury to do unnecessary things."

A moment passed as Jonas thoughtfully tapped his fingers on the tabletop. "Do you think that's good?"

Colleen's smile was wry. "Goodness doesn't enter into it, Mr. Dobbs."

His gray eyes traveled over her face. She was the most unpretentious woman he'd ever met. Even so, she was utterly feminine. In spite of her plain clothes, simple hairstyle and lack of makeup, she had a natural beauty that was quietly alluring. Her red-gold hair, cool green eyes and soft, petal-pink lips turned his thoughts far away from mortgages. He knew he would still be thinking of her after he left, and he wasn't happy with that idea at all.

Jonas drained his glass and reached for his hat. "Well, I'd better let you get on your way," he said, rising to his feet.

Colleen rose from her chair and watched him settle his hat over his dark hair. She still wasn't sure about his motives, but for the moment she would give him the benefit of the doubt. "Thank you for coming, Mr. Dobbs. I—I know that I owe the mortgages, but things have been rough the past few months. Dad's medical bills were—well, you're not interested in all of that," she said, her voice brusque. She swallowed, then forced a proud smile on her face. "But I will pay the loans. Be sure and tell Roger that."

Impulsively Jonas reached for her hand. He didn't know why, he just wanted to touch her, assure her in some way, or maybe it was to assure himself that touching her would be no different than touching any woman.

Colleen trembled inside as his big hand closed over hers. He'd shaken her hand before, but this was different. This wasn't a handshake. It was an intimate contact, reminding her that in spite of everything she was still a woman.

"If there's any way I can help you, Colleen, any way at all, just give me a call," he said, shocking himself and Colleen. He didn't know what had prompted the impulsive offer, but now that it was out he couldn't take it back.

She let out a long breath. "That's very nice of you, Mr. Dobbs. But I'll manage somehow."

"If determination is anything to go on, then I'm sure you will. But just in case you do run into problems, remember me, okay?"

Colleen was overwhelmed by his offer, but then she suddenly remembered he was a lawyer. Of course he wanted her to ask for help. That was the way the man made his living.

"I'll think about that," she said.

He smiled gently and released her hand. "Goodbye, Colleen, and good luck."

"Goodbye, Mr. Dobbs."

Jonas let himself out the kitchen door. Colleen watched him walk across the yard until he was out of sight. She was going to be late getting back to camp, but even knowing this, it was a struggle to motivate herself into action.

Jonas Dobbs's visit had left her gripped by thought. Not necessarily by the things he'd said, but more by the man himself. That scared Colleen. Men were dangerous. She'd learned that the hard way. And a man like Jonas Dobbs was probably the most dangerous kind of all.

Chapter Two

Colleen's luck was not going well. For the past two weeks she'd been trying to sell her old Chevrolet pickup through the classified ads and by phoning all the people she knew, but no one wanted to give her a decent price for it. True, it was twelve years old, but that didn't mean she wanted to give it away.

Today she'd driven in to Gunnison to try the used car lots. She doubted a car dealer would give her half the amount she needed for the truck, but her choices were quickly narrowing down to one or two.

Colleen wanted to pay the mortgages as quickly as possible. If she left them hanging for much longer the property would be listed publicly and then it would be too late. Roger or anyone could come along and purchase it. She had to take care of them somehow, someway.

Colleen stood out on the graveled parking lot as Red Pitman, a car dealer, walked around her faded red pickup.

"The tires are pretty threadbare," he said, kicking the right front. "And the dent on the hood needs to be fixed."

Colleen let out an impatient breath. She knew the truck wasn't in perfect shape, but it still ran well. "So what do you think you could give for it?" Colleen asked.

The older man rubbed his jaw as he studied the truck. "Well, I tell you, Miss McNair, we take trade-ins, we're not in the business of buying vehicles. But seeing you want rid of it, I'll make an exception and give you six hundred dollars."

Colleen simply stared at the man. "The motor alone is worth more than that!"

With a patronizing smile he folded his arms and rocked back on his heels. "That's probably true, but I'm in the business to make money. I've got to leave myself room for profit."

Yeah, a big one Colleen thought angrily. "Then I'm afraid I've just wasted your time and mine, Mr. Pitman. Because I could never let the truck go for that."

Colleen opened the door and climbed behind the wheel. Red Pitman walked up to the open window.

"You're making a big mistake, Miss McNair. You're not going to find another dealer that will give you a penny over that."

"I'd drive it to Slumgullian pass and push it over the cliff before I'd sell it for what you're offering," she said tightly.

She started the engine with a roar and rammed the gearshift in reverse. Without a glance at the car dealer, she began to maneuver the pickup out of the lot. As she was pulling out into the street a car suddenly blocked her path.

Colleen stomped on the brakes, spraying loose gravel from the tires. *Good Lord,* she thought, *what kind of idiot would do that?*

Cutting the motor, she jumped out of the truck. She didn't have time to wait around while someone made a car deal. She needed to take care of business and get back to her sheep.

Colleen was halfway to the familiar-looking car when the door swung open and Jonas Dobbs climbed out. He stood to his full height and Colleen stopped in her tracks. It was unnerving to come face-to-face with the man she'd thought of every day for the past two weeks.

"Hello, Colleen," he said with a disarming smile. "Sorry about pulling in front of you like that, but I wanted to catch you before you got out on the street."

Oh, God, she thought. He'd probably heard from Roger again. The bank had mailed her a letter yesterday, reminding her of the mortgages coming due in two weeks. Roger was no doubt ready to pounce on her land like a dog on a bone. "I was just trying to sell my truck to Mr. Pitman," she said. "Unfortunately we couldn't come to terms."

Jonas closed the last steps between them. "I saw your truck as I was passing by and wondered if you'd had any luck. I tried to call you a few days ago, but I discovered you didn't have a phone."

He'd tried to call her? She couldn't imagine him doing that unless it was to convey news of Roger's plans. "The phone lines aren't near enough to the farm for a telephone," she explained.

Her eyes strayed over to the truck. "Everyone I've tried to deal with wants me to practically give them the truck."

Jonas's smile was wry. "Well, that doesn't surprise me. Everyone wants something for nothing."

"I'm learning that the hard way," she said.

It was a sunny day. Gunnison felt hot compared to Colleen's mountain camp. She could feel perspiration dampening her cheeks and upper lip. She looked at Jonas to see if the summer heat was affecting him. He looked cool in his dark trousers and white shirt with the sleeves rolled up on his forearms. He was wearing a tie, but it was the western bola type, fashioned from silver and turquoise. He'd left his collar unbuttoned and the tie had been loosened. The casual style suited him, she thought. His looks were too rough and rangy for restrictive clothing.

Jonas's gaze traveled from the look of despair on Colleen's face to her white blouse and yellow printed skirt. The only time he'd seen her in a dress was at Roger's wedding, more than ten years ago. His curiosity about her legs was probably showing all over him, but he was a man after all, and Colleen's legs were definitely worth looking at.

Pulling his eyes back to her face, he said, "Let me have a look at the truck. I've been needing one for use on the ranch. It might be just what I'm looking for."

Colleen's eyes widened as Jonas began to inspect the truck. "I really doubt it, Mr. Dobbs. It's dented in places and the tires are bald."

He waved away her words as he walked around to the hood and released the latch. "I'm more concerned about the condition of the motor."

She joined him as he looked under the hood. "It runs well. But I don't think you'd want—"

"Start it up," he said, cutting off her protest.

Seeing he was serious, Colleen slid behind the wheel and started the motor.

"Give it a little gas," he said.

She gunned the motor slightly until he said, "That's good."

Colleen climbed back out to stand a few steps away from Jonas. Seconds later Red Pitman walked up to them.

"I offered Miss McNair a good deal, Jonas," he said. "She just doesn't seem to know a good price when she hears it."

Jonas shut the hood and turned to look at one of the town's most prominent car dealers.

"How much was that, Red?"

The man puffed out his barrel chest as though he resented Jonas's presence. "Six hundred dollars."

Colleen looked up at Jonas. She couldn't detect any change in his expression, making it impossible to tell what he thought about Red Pitman's offer.

Jonas turned to Colleen. "I'll give you twelve hundred dollars for the truck, Colleen. Do you think that's a fair price?"

Colleen was so staggered by his offer that for a moment she couldn't speak. "Mr. Dobbs, I—"

"Well, how about thirteen hundred?" Jonas went on.

Red Pitman spluttered and Colleen gasped. She didn't know why he was doing this, but she couldn't believe he actually intended to pay her thirteen hundred dollars for a battered old truck.

"Do you really want it?" she finally managed to ask.

He grimaced at her question. "Of course I want it."

"It's getting some years on it," she warned him.

"The motor sounds fine."

"You haven't even driven it," she reasoned.

He smiled at her. A nice, gentle smile that was an odd contrast to his rough-featured face.

"You drove it here, didn't you?"

She nodded, her mind whirling as she tried to figure out what he was about.

"That's good enough for me."

With a disgusted snort, Red Pitman turned and walked away. Colleen waited until the man was out of earshot then said, "Okay, Mr. Dobbs, he's gone now, you can quit the act."

Jonas's heavy brows arched quizzically at Colleen. "Act? I thought we were making a truck sale."

Color flooded Colleen's cheeks. "I'm sure you were just saying all that for Red Pitman's benefit. You couldn't possibly want my truck—not for that amount of money."

He patted the hood of the pickup. "Of course I want the truck. Let's park our vehicles out of the way and walk down the street. I'll write you a check while we have a cup of coffee."

Arguing any further would only make her look like an idiot. "All right," she reluctantly agreed.

After they moved off the car lot and parked the vehicles along the street, Jonas guided her down the sidewalk.

"Colleen, you should have known better than to try to sell your truck to a dealer, especially Pitman. He's a skinflint."

They were walking side by side. Every now and then his arm brushed against Colleen's. She was far too aware of his touch.

"I've tried for the past two weeks to sell the truck, without any luck. Car dealers were my last choice."

"Two weeks isn't enough time to sell a vehicle."

Without looking at him, she said, "My time is running out, Mr. Dobbs."

There was a small café directly across the street from them. They waited for the traffic light to change, then crossed and entered the restaurant.

It was late afternoon. As Jonas guided her to a small table near a window overlooking the street, Colleen looked around the room. It was decorated western-style. Ranching scenes done in oils were hanging here and there on the walls. At the far end was an enormous set of steer horns mounted over a mirror. Colleen caught a glimpse of her reflection as she took a seat on a wooden chair. She looked pale and strained. But that was not surprising. She hadn't planned on doing business today with Jonas Dobbs.

"Two coffees," Jonas said as a waitress approached their table.

The woman nodded and moved away to get their order. Jonas turned his attention to Colleen. "So, who's watching the sheep while you're in town?"

"My dog," Colleen answered, then lowered her eyes to the tabletop. "You know, you can still back out of the deal. I'll understand."

"But I don't understand why I'd want to. I told you I needed the truck," Jonas said.

"I don't really think so," Colleen said quietly.

Jonas chuckled and Colleen lifted her eyes back up to him. He smiled at her.

"Then why am I buying it?" he asked.

Colleen shrugged and brushed her bangs away from her eyes. Lord, she wanted to be cool in front of this man, but she was finding it very difficult. He was too much of a man, too laid-back and content with his position in life. Colleen felt like a backwoods hillbilly compared to him. "I haven't figured that out yet."

Jonas watched an array of conflicting emotions pass across her face and wondered what she was really thinking. But then, what was he really thinking? He was pushing his way into her affairs and he didn't want to ask himself why. "There's nothing to figure out," he said, much more casually than he was feeling. "I can use the truck and you can use the money. The way I see it, we've helped each other."

It would certainly help Colleen, but as far as Jonas was concerned she doubted the deal would benefit him in any way. She had the oddest feeling that he was doing the whole thing to help her. But for the life of her Colleen couldn't imagine why.

The waitress arrived with the coffee. Colleen sipped hers while Jonas pulled out his wallet and began filling out a check.

"You haven't heard from Roger, have you?" he asked.

Colleen's hand froze in midair at the unexpected question. "No. Have you?"

Jonas shook his head. "Not since I called and told him you said no sale. Frankly, he wasn't too surprised by the news. But he's still confident you'll be forced to sell, and he's willing to offer a price you won't be able to refuse."

"So he thinks. But what he doesn't know is that I'd rather die than see Roger get my land," she muttered, then lowered her coffee cup back to the table. "The mortgages are due the week after next. That's why I've been in such a hurry to sell the truck."

Jonas signed his name with an authoritative flourish then pushed the check over to Colleen. "Will this be enough to take care of them?"

Colleen felt herself blushing. It was embarrassing to have this man know of her financial plight. "Not hardly. But it will help."

Jonas watched her eyes drop away from him and her fingers quaver as she reached for the handle on her coffee cup. It was obvious she was desperately trying to hold on to her composure. She was also alone and in need. He wished that she wouldn't view him as a lawyer or stranger. He wished she would reach across the table, cling to his hand and ask for his help. *Good Lord, Jonas,* he silently scolded himself. *You're a lawyer, why can't you look at her like any other person that comes to you in need?* But the fact was, every time he looked at Colleen he only saw the woman.

"I hope you're still not thinking of selling the sheep," he said. "I don't think that would be a wise idea. Not if you intend to continue to make a living from them."

Colleen breathed deeply then lifted her eyes back to his. There was such a look of genuine concern on his face that it was difficult to mistake it for anything else.

"I don't really have much choice in the matter. I have nothing else left to sell. I'm hoping it won't take more than half the flock. Besides," she added with a resigned shrug. "It doesn't take that much income for me to live on."

No, it probably didn't, he thought. Not the way she lived. The money she spent was more than likely just for groceries and utilities. He doubted very seriously that she spent much on clothes or entertainment.

"I don't suppose you've had second thoughts about selling the place and moving into town?"

Something close to panic filled her green eyes. "Never! I don't belong here. I wouldn't be happy."

Jonas wondered if she was happy now, but it was difficult to tell what a woman like Colleen defined as happiness. She seemed to want little and ask for nothing. It intrigued him that she was so guarded with herself and her emotions. For probably the hundredth time since he'd first seen her out on the mountain, he wondered what had made her that way.

"Well," he said with a brief smile, "you should know that better than anyone."

Colleen let out a breath of relief. At least he wasn't going to pursue the idea of her selling the land. She picked up her coffee and sipped carefully.

"The property has been in my family for several generations. I hate to think that now it has finally been handed down to me, I'll lose it."

Jonas hardly saw it that way. Roger had been right about one thing: old man McNair had lived like a hermit for years, not really caring if the place prospered. He was the one who'd put the farm in jeopardy, not Colleen. But obviously she didn't see it that way.

"I can understand your wanting to pass it down to your own children someday in years to come. But right now you should consider your own needs, Colleen."

Colleen's face grew very pale, making Jonas wonder what kind of nerve he'd struck. It was almost on the tip of his tongue to ask if he'd offended her, when he saw her features harden in a way he'd never expected to see on a young woman like her.

"I don't imagine I'll be having children. So that's not really a consideration."

Her voice was sharp and decisive, as though she'd decided the way of her life long ago, and nothing was going to interrupt that course. Jonas thought it very sad. She didn't intend to have children in her life. Did that mean she wasn't planning on having a man in her life, either? He couldn't imagine her living the rest of her life alone. But then there were those that couldn't imagine him wanting to live the rest of *his* life without a wife.

Colleen nervously picked up the check, folded it in the middle then put it safely away in her purse. Her coffee cup was nearly empty and she was ready to go. She needed to get away from this man with his questions and probing gray eyes.

"I really should be getting back to the farm," she said. "It's already past three."

Jonas drank the last of his coffee and placed the cup back on its saucer. "I was thinking if you could follow me to my ranch and drop off the truck then I could take you back to your farm. You do have something else to drive?" he asked.

Colleen had forgotten all about delivering the truck to his place. All of her thoughts had been concentrated on getting away from Jonas Dobbs and back to her home where it was safe, quiet, secluded. But now it looked as though she would have to be in his company for at least another hour or two.

"Yes, I have a Jeep," she answered as they both rose to their feet. "Are you sure you have time for this? If you have clients waiting for you, I can always bring the truck to you later."

He shook his head. "I'm finished for the day. No problem."

Nodding, Colleen followed him. After pausing to pay the cashier for the coffee, Jonas pushed open the door and allowed Colleen to precede him out onto the sidewalk.

The air felt warm and natural after being in the air-conditioned café. Colleen breathed deeply, glad to be out of the café and at least more than an arm's length from Jonas Dobbs.

"You do know where I live?" he asked when they were back at the pickup and car they'd left parked along the street.

Colleen nodded. Even though she rarely made trips to town, she did know where the big Dobbs ranch was located. After all, the back side of it connected with her sheep ranch. However, since it was probably the biggest spread in the area, that made his house miles from hers. It also made her wonder why Jonas had become a lawyer when he could have easily lived off the ranch. "Yes, I'll follow you," she told him.

Jonas slid behind the wheel of his car and Colleen climbed in the pickup that had now become Jonas's, and prepared to back out into the street.

For more than ten miles, Colleen followed Jonas at a close distance, then turned behind him as he drove under a sign arched across a drive. Tall, white letters spelled out: Slash D Ranch.

Over a quarter of a mile long, it was an ominous drive, straight as an arrow and lined on either side by tall blue spruces. When they reached the end of it, Jonas pulled to a stop in front of a massive house built in rock and natural wood that had been stained a deep brown color. It was L-shaped and possessed at least three levels built into the side of the mountain. Spruce, aspens and cottonwoods grew close to the house, shading a wide sun deck on the west side. The deck was adorned with potted geraniums and pansies and white wicker furniture.

Colleen couldn't imagine living in such beautiful surroundings. She sat examining it closely as she waited for Jonas to come over and tell her where to park the truck.

More than likely he'd want to take it down to the barns, she thought. It looked like a piece of junk compared to everything else. But she was wrong. When he walked up to the truck he surprised her, saying, "Just leave it here in the drive, Colleen. I'll want to tinker with it when I get back, anyway."

Nodding, she shut off the motor and climbed out of the truck. "I have the truck's registration in my handbag," she told him. "Let me sign it and give it to you before I forget."

"Let's go into the house," he suggested. "You can do it while I check my answering machine."

Colleen hung back as he started up the steps. She didn't want to go inside with Jonas. She felt very out of place and uncomfortable, not only with the house, but also with Jonas. She knew he had done nothing to warrant that feeling in her. He'd been very kind to her by giving her an exceptional price for the truck. But still, she could not help remembering a time long ago when a young man had invited her into his home. Once she'd gone inside her life had been changed traumatically.

Jonas glanced back over his shoulder to see her lingering beside the pickup. "It's all right, Colleen. I live here alone, since my mother took a house in town, so there's no one around to bite you, 'cause I don't bite," he added with a grin.

His teasing eased her wariness somewhat. She moved away from the truck and joined him on the steps. The steps and the shallow porch were also wooden, stained to match the house. Flowerpots were here too, and Colleen silently identified pink impatiens and white petunias.

"Your house is very beautiful, Mr. Dobbs," she murmured as they walked up to the front entrance.

"Thank you, Colleen. My father built it himself. It was one of his best achievements, he used to say."

"Used to?"

He nodded ruefully. "He died of a stroke a few years ago. I still miss the old coot. We were the best of friends."

So now it was only him and his mother, she thought. That answered her earlier conjecture as to whether he was married, and somehow that answer didn't surprise her. What surprised her was the peculiar feeling of relief running through her.

"I'm sure you do," she murmured. She and her father couldn't have been called the best of friends. But she missed him just the same. Her throat thick, she merely nodded.

Jonas glanced down and caught the poignant expression on her face. "I'm sorry, Colleen. Of course you miss your father, too. It must be terribly lonely for you now."

He could never know. Nor would anyone know how completely alone she felt. How much at times she missed and longed for human companionship.

"Yes," she said simply. "It does get lonely."

They entered a small foyer. Colleen could see a formal sitting room off to the left, but before she had a chance to see anything else, he guided her down a long hallway.

"The answering machine is in the den," he explained as they walked. "There's a powder room just to the right, if you'd like to freshen up before the drive to your place."

"Yes, I would. Thank you," she told him.

He went into the den and Colleen entered the bathroom. Her feet instantly sank into a deep rose carpet and she found herself standing in front of a long, beautifully fixtured vanity cabinet. A lighted mirror covered the wall in front of her, flashing her image back at her.

After making use of the facilities, she applied a bit of pink lipstick and stood back to look at herself. Her blouse was threatening to ride out of the waistband of her skirt, and she quickly straightened it, then pulled a comb from her purse and ran it through her short hair.

She thought she looked younger than twenty-five—or maybe just more naive than she should be at her age. That was probably how Jonas saw her: a naive young woman who knew nothing about the outside world. The thought was a solemn reminder to Colleen, and she quickly turned away from the mirror and left the room.

When Colleen stepped quietly into the den, Jonas was on the phone. She stood just inside the door, not knowing whether to take a seat and wait, or go back outside to allow him to finish his conversation in private.

She was turning to leave when Jonas spotted her. Putting his hand over the phone he said, "Sit down, Colleen. I won't be but a minute."

Reluctantly she turned back and took a seat on a long leather couch. Jonas was sitting at the far end of the room where an enormous desk was situated by a row of long windows. At the opposite end of the room was a wide rock fireplace flanked by leather armchairs.

It was a comfortable room, one that fit Jonas perfectly. She could easily picture him here in the winter, in front of a roaring fire, mulling over a law case or a cattle deal. It was a long cry from her cold drafty house, where she was forced to dress in layers of insulated underwear and struggled to keep three of the rooms heated to a bearable temperature.

Colleen realized Jonas had put down the phone and was rising from the desk. Quickly she reached in her handbag for the registration papers. "Do you have a pen?" she asked.

Jonas pulled one out of a cup on the desk before crossing the room.

"I don't really know where to sign. Maybe you'd better look it over." Sitting rigidly on the edge of the couch, she handed the papers to him.

Jonas took them and sat down beside her. Colleen's heartbeat fluttered weakly in her breast. He was so close she could practically feel the length of his thigh against hers. She wanted desperately to jump up and run away from him and the peculiar feelings he aroused in her.

"Very simple," he said, as he studied the papers. "Just sign one time on this line, and put the date just to the right."

Leaning toward her, he pointed to the exact spot. Colleen could feel her insides shaking and she wondered if she'd be able to sign her name legibly.

"Yes, I see," she murmured. Gripping the pen, she quickly scratched her name across the line then thrust the form back at him.

Jonas took it but didn't make a move to leave her side. Instead, to Colleen's dismay, he reached over and took her hand from her lap. The contact forced her to lift her eyes up to his.

"Colleen," he said quietly, his gray eyes probing her face, "I have the feeling that you don't want to talk about your problem with the mortgages, but before we go, I wish that you would. I have a feeling that you need help. You say the banks won't make you a loan. Well, I'm offering you one. Whatever amount you need, just name it and I'll write you another check."

Colleen gasped, and for a moment her eyes locked with his. Her breath stopped somewhere between her lungs and her throat. Then, as the full impact of his words sank in, she jerked her hand away from his. "No—no I could never do that. It's not—this is my problem. I'll work it out myself."

Jonas knew she was right. It was her problem, not his. But something was pushing him toward her. He wanted to say it was because he was a compassionate man, but deep down he knew compassion had nothing to do with it. It was simpler than that: he was attracted to Colleen McNair. And he also had an idea of what it felt like to have the threat of having his land taken away. Combine the two, and it was a volatile mixture. Attraction and compassion could get a man in trouble, especially with an independent woman like Colleen. His face full of frustration, he said, "I'm offering you an easy way to work things out. It's that simple."

There was nothing simple about any of this, she thought, and the shaking that had started inside Colleen the moment he'd sat down beside her now increased twofold. "Yes—yes, I know. But I wouldn't feel right by taking it." Her eyes questioned him. "I can't understand why you're even offering the loan. You hardly know me. Why would you risk money on me?"

An enigmatic smile lifted the corners of his mouth. Damned if he could—or would—answer her question. He only knew that every time he looked at her something inside of him turned to putty. And maybe he could help her save her land, if not his own. But no, he thought, the best thing for him to do would be to tell her goodbye once and for all. The words, however, wouldn't come out of his mouth. Instead, he said, "Risks usually pay off."

That was exactly what Colleen was afraid of. If she did take his money, he would expect something in return, something she wouldn't be able to give.

Jumping quickly to her feet she moved away from him and the couch. "I—I have no collateral," she said in a breathless rush.

"Yes, you do," he insisted. "Your sheep are fine collateral."

Shrugging, she turned her back on him. It would be so easy to say yes, that she would take his money, she thought. The worries over losing her land would be gone, but they would be replaced by the worry of being mortgaged to Jonas Dobbs. She couldn't place herself in such a compromising situation, not even to him.

"Anything can happen to sheep," she argued. "A disease could sweep through the flock and take them all."

"That's highly unlikely."

Colleen turned back around to face him. He was an imposing figure of a man.

"It's very generous of you, Mr. Dobbs. But I could never accept your money."

"You'd rather lose your land?"

She shook her head vehemently, making the tiny drops of amber in her ears dance against her neck. "I won't lose my land, even if I have to sell all the sheep!"

Jonas clucked his tongue in a disapproving manner. "You are one stubborn woman, Colleen."

She breathed in deeply. "My father taught me to be independent. It's just the way I am."

Yes, Jonas had already decided as much. Lana had been the same way. Determined, independent. She'd wound up hurting him more than he cared to admit. So why would he even let himself near another woman of that sort, he wondered, much less entangle himself in her affairs. Frowning at his own weakness he said, "Yes, I can see that. I can also see that I'm not making any headway with this, so we might as well be on our way. But I'm still leaving the option open for the loan. If you don't come up with the money between now and the middle of next week, all you have to do is call."

Colleen picked up her handbag from the couch. "Thank you for the offer, Mr. Dobbs, but I won't be calling."

On the drive to her house she sat quietly, staring out the window as the winding highway carried them deeper into the mountains. Clouds were gathering over the snow-capped peaks. Soon lightning was streaking down in jagged bolts all around them. Almost every evening thunderstorms poured down on the mountains for an hour or two. It was the way of summer in the Rockies, one that Colleen was very accustomed to.

Darkness had nearly arrived by the time they reached Colleen's house. Rain was still falling, although the lightning and thunder were now just a faint rumble in the distance.

Jonas parked the car close to the house, then turned to face Colleen. "You're not going out to your camp tonight, are you?"

She remembered that he'd asked her the same thing the last time he'd been here. "Yes. I'd worry about Dangit and the sheep if I didn't."

"I worry about you, Colleen."

He worried about her! Colleen was so taken aback by his statement she didn't know what to say. "That's rather hard for me to believe. You never worried about me before."

His serious expression didn't alter as he continued to study her face. "I didn't know you before. Not really know you. I didn't realize you were still living here until I read your father's obituary."

Colleen felt as if his gray eyes were caressing her. It was such a disturbing feeling that her heart wasn't sure if it wanted to stop completely or run a race. Swallowing, she said, "You don't really know me now, Mr. Dobbs."

His hand reached over and touched her shoulder. "I'll never get to know you if you keep calling me Mr. Dobbs," he said, his voice low and husky.

Even though his touch wasn't a sexual one, it stirred Colleen down to her toes, and she had the strongest urge to close her eyes. "You'll always be Mr. Dobbs to me," she managed to say.

"Don't you think you're being rather hard on me?"

A fleeting smile touched her lips. "I'm not used to being with people, Mr. Dobbs. Sheep and dogs are my companions. I guess I've forgotten how to relate to other humans. Or how to trust them," she added, wondering why she felt the need to explain herself to him.

His brows lifted with surprise. "Surely you trust me by now, Colleen. Or do you still think I'm in with Roger to get your land?"

Dropping her head, she murmured, "I'm not sure. Maybe you'd rather have Roger owning the land next to yours than me."

Jonas sighed heavily. "Look Colleen, I know what kind of neighbor you are. You'd never do anything to jeopardize your land or my land. Roger hasn't said why he wants the property. So it's just common sense for me to want to keep things as they are."

"You're a persuasive man," she said, looking back up at him. "You must be very successful in the courtroom."

A half smile curled his lips. "You think so, huh?"

Colleen felt breathless as she watched the sexy smile transform his craggy features. "Well, you almost have me believing you."

"Almost," he repeated. "Almost isn't quite what I wanted, but for now I'll settle for it." Pulling his hand away from her shoulder, he reached for the gearshift. "I'd better be getting back to the ranch."

Colleen didn't know whether to be relieved or sad that he was finally leaving. Her shoulder still tingled from his touch and for one reckless second she wondered what it would be like to kiss him.

Trying to disregard that idea, she said in a quick rush, "Thank you for buying the truck, Mr. Dobbs. I hope you'll be able to get some use from it."

With a sidelong glance, he said, "I'm sure I will. Goodbye, Colleen."

Jonas watched her scramble out of the car, realizing as he did that he was reluctant to leave her. He didn't know why. She obviously didn't want his company or his help. Hell, she wouldn't even call him by his first name. Even so, he didn't like to think of her alone. He'd rather think of her in his arms, all warm and soft, and yielding. Just the idea of it brought an urgent need inside him.

"Goodbye, Mr. Dobbs." She clicked the door shut on the car, then without looking back she dashed through the rain to the house.

Jonas waited until she was safely inside before he put the car into reverse and backed out onto the dirt road.

From inside, Colleen watched Jonas's car disappear into the rainy twilight. She still carried the image of him behind the driver's wheel and could easily imagine him as he drove back over the winding mountain road. Strong, long-legged, a thoughtful expression on his dark face.

Chapter Three

"Yoohoo—Colleen? Are you up there?"

Colleen was gathering firewood when she heard the familiar sound of her friend's voice. Quickly she moved out into the open and waved at the woman.

"Come on up," Colleen called back down the mountainside.

Inez started the climb up and Colleen carried her armful of dead wood over to camp and stacked it next to the tent. It was late afternoon and the shadows were lengthening. It was a quiet time of the day and she was happy to see her old friend. She'd much rather visit with Inez than sit and stew over her financial problems.

The plump brunette was breathing heavily by the time she reached Colleen's camp. "What are you doing up here, Colleen," she gasped, "trying to give me a heart attack?"

Laughing, Colleen offered the only camp chair to Inez. "Here. Sit down before you fall down."

Inez collapsed into the folding chair. Colleen sat down on the ground and waited for her friend to catch her breath. The woman was dressed in a neon green sweater and black capri pants. Golden hoops dangled beneath her bushy hair. She was outgoing and flamboyant, the complete opposite of Colleen.

"There's grass at the base of the mountain that those blasted sheep of yours could eat!"

Colleen smiled patiently at her friend's observation. "Yes, but the sheep eat high up on the mountain, too. My camp's a happy medium between the two," Colleen explained.

"Happy medium! I'm about to get a nosebleed!"

"Well, I'm glad you decided to come out for a visit. Even if the climb has endangered your health," Colleen said jokingly.

By now Inez had regained her breath and was looking at Colleen with thoughtful concern. "How've you been, sweetie?"

Without looking at Inez, Colleen shrugged. "Fine."

"We haven't seen you in a long time. Bob and I were beginning to worry about you."

"No need to worry. Dangit and I have been watching the sheep. Sometimes they watch us back. There's not too much else that goes on out here."

Inez frowned. "You would say that. Any day I expect a forest ranger to come into town and say they've found you half-eaten by a bear."

Colleen chuckled. Being eaten by a bear was the least of her worries. "Don't worry, Inez. A bear wouldn't like the taste of me. I'd be too tough and stringy."

Inez made an exasperated gesture with her hands. "Go ahead and joke about it. But one of these days you're going to need help out here and no one will be around. That's when I'm going to kick myself for not making you quit this craziness."

"You couldn't make me quit ranching if you stuck a shotgun to my head," Colleen told her.

Inez grimaced. "Colleen, you know how busy I am in the restaurant during the summer. I could give you all the work you wanted."

Inez owned a restaurant in Lake City, a mountain village thirty miles south, nestled deep in the mountains near Lake San Cristobal. During the summer it was overrun with tourists, but in the winter it was almost a ghost town. During that time only seventy or eighty people stayed in town and braved the deep snow and cabin fever.

"But I wouldn't have a job in the winter to tide me over. And besides, I wouldn't like cooking or waitressing. Not when I can be out here in the fresh air with animals that don't demand or complain like your customers sometimes do."

"Well, you do have me there," Inez agreed. "Just when the beautiful weather arrives I have to spend it in the kitchen cooking. One of these days I'm going to win a sweepstakes and retire."

Colleen chuckled, then asked, "How about a cup of coffee?"

"Sounds good. Can I help?"

Getting to her feet, Colleen stirred the ashes of the campfire. There were a few glowing coals left from an earlier fire. She tossed on a piece of kindling and waited until it flared to life before adding a couple of sticks of firewood. "You do enough cooking," Colleen insisted. "Just sit there and tell me how you got away from the restaurant today."

Inez sighed and crossed her legs at the ankles. "Easy. I just took off my apron and told Bob I'd had all I could stand. He and the other girls can make it without me for a while."

Bob was Inez's husband. The couple were both in their mid-thirties and had moved from Texas to Lake City ten years before. Colleen had known them nearly that long and considered them both good friends. They'd helped all they could while her father had been ill. Inez was one of the few people who really knew Colleen, and Colleen regarded Inez as the one person she could confide in. Yet between Colleen's sheep and Inez's restaurant they rarely had a chance to visit.

With the coffee makings put together, Colleen placed the pot on a grate above the fire. She was taking her seat on the ground when Dangit came bounding into camp.

He lapped affectionately at Colleen's face then wiggled and twisted over to Inez, who crooned and made a big fuss over him.

"I sold the pickup," Colleen said as Inez petted the dog.

Inez's eye widened with interest. "Oh. Did you get what you were asking?"

An uncomfortable warmth filled Colleen's cheeks as she thought of Jonas. "More."

"More! You're kidding, aren't you?"

Colleen shook her head. "No."

"Who bought it? Anyone I know?"

Colleen busily prodded the fire. "I don't know if you know him or not. It was Jonas Dobbs."

"Dobbs. Dobbs?" Inez repeated thoughtfully. "Isn't that the guy that owns the big ranch south of Gunnison? Part of it connects with your land, doesn't it?"

Colleen nodded. "Jonas is a lawyer."

"How in the world did you manage to sell the truck to him?"

"It's a long story. I was at Pitman's car lot when Jonas drove up. He more than doubled the amount Pitman offered for the truck. I could hardly refuse it."

"Not unless you were crazy," Inez agreed.

The coffee began to boil. Colleen took it off the flame then reached for two cups. After filling both she handed one to Inez.

"Well, Jonas said he needed a used truck for the ranch. It will serve that purpose."

Inez cradled the cup in her hands and blew at the hot liquid. "You call him Jonas. Do you know him?"

The flush on Colleen's cheeks deepened and she turned her face toward the fire, away from her friend. She hadn't realized that she'd called him Jonas. She'd done it naturally. Colleen supposed it was because in her thoughts he was always Jonas, not Mr. Dobbs.

"Not well. I met him years ago. He was a friend of Roger's. Sometimes they would come out and hike the mountains behind our house."

Inez made a face at the mention of Colleen's cousin. "I can't imagine you doing business with a friend of Roger's. I thought you'd learned your lesson about that years ago."

Colleen's features hardened as she stared at the small flames of the campfire. "Jonas doesn't appear to be like Roger. Leastwise, on the surface. Jonas is the one who let me know that Roger wanted to buy my land, but he says he's not legally representing him."

This information had Inez's eyes narrowing keenly at Colleen's downbent head. "Do you believe him?"

Colleen shrugged and took a sip of her coffee. "It doesn't really matter if I believe Jonas or not, because I have no intention of selling."

"Hmm. It sure makes me wonder. Two old friends. Land that connects. Sounds like they're in cahoots."

For some reason Colleen didn't want to believe Jonas could do that to her. It hurt to think he might see her only as an obstacle in the way. Sighing, she said, "I don't know about Jonas. I only know that I've got to come up with another hunk of money in three days' time or I can forget about this place. Once the bank takes possession of the land Roger will pounce on it like a cat on a rat."

"Three days! My God, Colleen. What are you doing out here? You should be over at Gunnison seeing a banker!"

Colleen's laugh was sharp and brittle. "Why waste my time with a banker? They'd hardly loan money to a woman who can't even make enough money to pay her old loans."

Inez cast her a worried look. "What are you going to do?"

Colleen's expression was flat as she looked back at Inez. "I know what I *have* to do. Tomorrow I'm going to take a survey of the flock, then get in touch with a sheep buyer."

Colleen didn't know why she'd been putting it off. She knew the sheep had to be sold. Maybe deep down she'd just been hoping for a miracle to come along.

"Look Colleen, Bob and I have some money put away. We could—"

Colleen quickly shook her head. "I'd never dream of it. That's your savings for retirement."

"Yes, but—"

"But nothing. It's not your fault that Dad was—" She couldn't finish. Didn't know how to finish. She couldn't call her father shiftless, because he hadn't actually been lazy. He'd just been a man who'd been content with only the bare necessities of life. He'd thought the working rat race was crazy, and that God intended the human race to be satisfied with simple things.

He'd never wanted Colleen to go to college or get out in the world. And when she'd tried and wound up being hurt in the process, it had only strengthened his beliefs. After that, Colleen had accepted her father's ways, because on one hand he'd been right, and on the other she'd been filled with too much guilt to go against his will a second time.

"Your father was a good man, Colleen. His values were different from other people's, that's all."

Colleen blinked at the tears burning the back of her eyes. Gripping her mug of coffee with both hands, she brought it up to her mouth and gulped at the scalding liquid. She didn't want to cry in front of Inez. She didn't want her to know how lost and alone she really felt.

"I know," Colleen said huskily. "But sometimes I get so frustrated when I remember how he was and—and the mortgages. Why did he leave me like this? Didn't he care about me, or my welfare?"

"He loved you," Inez answered. "But we both know that material security was not one of his concerns. I guess he figured you'd take care of yourself somehow."

A few moments of silence passed as Colleen thought about her friend's words. Inez was right. Her father had always had the attitude that, left alone, things would somehow take care of themselves.

"Well, enough about me. Tell me what's been going on over in Lake City," Colleen asked. "Lots of tourists now?"

Inez sighed. "Droves of them. We ran completely out of steaks last night. Fortunately the delivery truck arrived this morning. Oh, and Betsy Carlton is getting married to that man who took over the Alta Vista guest lodge. And, of course, everyone in town is getting ready for the big street dance on the fourth of July. Are you coming over?"

Colleen tilted her head in contemplation. "Maybe. If I get things squared away. I could help you in the kitchen."

"Kitchen!" Inez burst out. "We're going to forget the kitchen. We're going to dance and enjoy the music."

Colleen stood up. "Leave me out on the dancing part. I don't know how to and I don't want to know. I'll just listen to the band. You can dance for the both of us."

"Colleen," Inez groaned, "you're young and beautiful. When are you—"

Before she could finish the question, Colleen turned and walked a few steps away. She knew the argument Inez was about to start. They'd had it many times before. "You know how I feel about men, Inez. Please don't say anything else."

Seconds later Colleen felt Inez's fingers gently squeezing her shoulder. "I'd better go, sweetie. It's getting late and Bob will be worried if I'm much after dark."

Colleen turned around and briefly hugged Inez's shoulders. "I'm glad you came out to see me. And I'll try my best to make it over on the fourth."

Inez gave her an encouraging smile. "We'll be looking for you."

The women exchanged goodbyes and Colleen watched Inez scramble back down the mountainside to her car.

Dangit barked when the motor started and the car pulled away. Colleen leaned over and stroked the collie's head. "I know it's quiet now that she's gone, but we'll survive, Dangit."

We have to, she thought sadly. It was the only goal she had in life. Simple survival.

The next morning Colleen was up at the crack of dawn. After she and Dangit ate breakfast, the two of them headed out to find the sheep.

Colleen discovered the flock not far away, across a ravine and up the side of another mountain. Once she reached them, she took note of their condition and did a head count. It had been a while since she'd looked in the newspaper at the livestock prices. Colleen didn't know exactly what price sheep were going for at this time. She only hoped that by the time she sold enough to pay the mortgages, she'd have enough remaining to build another herd.

For the past few days Jonas's offer for a loan had hung in the back of her mind like a dark curtain. It was a temptation that pulled at her constantly, especially throughout the long nights when Colleen lay awake wondering, thinking, worrying.

Yet in her calmer moments, she knew taking money from Jonas would only double her troubles instead of getting her out of them. She would eventually have to pay him back, and looking down the road a year or even two years from now, she couldn't see her making that kind of profit. No, her only choice was to sell the sheep and try her best to start over.

Colleen was sitting on a rock watching the sheep graze when she noticed the sky beginning to grow dark with rain clouds. It was a surprise to see them since it wasn't yet noon and normally they didn't begin to gather over the mountains until four or five in the evening.

Quickly getting to her feet, she called to Dangit and headed back to camp. The two of them had barely made it down into the ravine when the rain and lightning hit. Without a slicker, she was soaked to the skin in a matter of seconds. At an elevation of over eight thousand feet, the rain was cold. Colleen was shivering and chilled to the bone by the time she reached camp.

The fire had long since been doused by the rain. Colleen went inside the tent and stripped off the sopping clothes, then wrapped herself in a blanket to warm herself.

Her hair was soaked and rivulets of water ran from her bangs, down her nose, and onto her cheeks and neck. Too cold to bring her arms out of the blanket to towel her hair dry, Colleen sat there shivering, listening to the sound of the storm.

The rain stopped long before Colleen felt warm enough to venture from the blanket and dress in dry clothes. But it was something she had to do. The day was slipping by and she still had to drive to the nearest phone to contact the sheep buyer. It would take him a day or two to come out and get the animals. She couldn't waste any more time.

Some fifteen miles away at her nearest neighbors, the Johnsons, Colleen used the telephone then drove back to her camp. The elderly couple had tried to persuade her to stay for supper, but she'd politely declined.

She honestly hadn't been hungry. In fact, now that she was back at the camp, she wasn't in the mood to cook supper or even sit out by the campfire. Colleen put her feelings down to depression. It was a sad realization that she was giving up her animals. They were more than her income. They were a constant part of her life. Once they were gone, it would be just her and Dangit.

Trying her best to shrug off her despair, she went inside the tent and turned on a battery-operated light. After undressing, she donned a thick cotton gown and slid into her bedroll.

A novel was lying beside her pillow and she reached for it, hoping the story would take her mind off her worries.

Yet tonight she felt so lethargic she couldn't enjoy her reading. After four pages she realized it was impossible to concentrate on the story. She put the book aside and switched off the light.

Through the flap of the tent, she could see the night sky had cleared and stars were shining down on the mountain tops. Just a few feet away Dangit lay guarding Colleen even more closely than he guarded the flock.

The only sound was the rushing of the stream a few yards away. Colleen nestled her head on the pillow and listened. Thoughts of Jonas filled her mind. She knew he wouldn't approve of her calling the sheep buyer. But then she'd probably never see him again anyway, so it wouldn't really matter.

Minutes later Colleen fell into an exhausted sleep only to awake hours later with a raging thirst and a scratchy throat. She kept a thermos of water beside her bed. Propping herself up on one elbow, she drank two cupfuls before putting the lid back on.

An aspirin would probably have made her feel better, since she was sure she was probably coming down with a cold. But her first aid kit was in the Jeep and she didn't relish the idea of getting up in the cold night air.

The next time Colleen woke it was well past sunup, which was a shock in itself because she never slept late. Dangit had crawled into the tent with her and was whining in her face.

"Dangit, what are you doing in here, boy?" she asked the dog.

Her voice came out sounding as weak and groggy as she felt. When she lifted her hand to stroke the dog's head it fell limply back against the covers.

Dangit whined and nudged her cheek with his wet nose, rousing Colleen again.

"I can't get up, Dangit. I'm too tired. Too sleepy..."

Her voice trailed away as she sank back into restless oblivion.

Jonas climbed the mountain slowly, scanning the green slopes for a sign of Colleen. She wasn't sitting outside the tent, nor was she near the sheep that were grazing among a stand of aspens some hundred yards to the left. The collie she called Dangit was not to be seen either, and a strange prickle of unease ran down Jonas's spine.

"Colleen? Are you here?" he called, once he reached the camp.

When there was no answer Jonas bent down and looked through the tent opening. Colleen was huddled under the covers, obviously unaware of his presence.

"Colleen?" Her name came out with soft surprise. Quickly he kneeled down and entered the tent.

The dog was lying beside her. His intelligent brown eyes traveled from Colleen to Jonas as if to convey that something was wrong with his mistress, but he wasn't quite sure he could trust Jonas to come near her.

"It's all right, boy," he said to the dog in a gentle voice. "I'm not going to hurt her."

The dog whined and thumped his tail. Jonas drew closer to Colleen, who was lying with her back to him.

"Colleen? Can you hear me?"

She didn't respond and he quickly turned her face around to him. It was flushed and the skin beneath his fingers was hot and dry.

Frightened and angry, Jonas wondered how many days would she have lain there with no one knowing she was ill if he hadn't come out to see her. For God's sake, why was she so intent on living like this? And why did he feel so responsible for her?

Grasping her shoulder he gave it a shake. "Colleen, it's Jonas. Wake up."

Colleen groaned and forced her heavy eyelids to lift. The image in front of her face swam in and out of her vision.

"Jonas?" she said weakly. "What are you doing here?"

"You're sick. I'm taking you to town."

Even though Colleen was disoriented with fever, there was something in Jonas's voice that told her she had no choice in the matter. She was too weak to argue anyway. It didn't matter to Colleen where he took her, as long as she could sleep.

The next time she woke she found herself in a hospital room. A doctor was listening to her chest with a stethoscope and she had the most horrible urge to cough.

"So I see you've decided to join us," the grayheaded doctor said to her.

"What is—" Her question was stopped by a racking cough that robbed her of breath.

Jonas, who'd been standing by the wall watching anxiously while the doctor examined Colleen, went quickly to her side.

"Is she getting pneumonia, Doctor?" Jonas asked, his eyes darting from Colleen to the doctor.

Colleen continued to cough and the doctor motioned for Jonas to help him lift her to a sitting position.

"I believe Miss McNair has developed a case of bronchitis," he said, then placed the stethoscope against Colleen's back and instructed her to breathe deeply. "Does that hurt?"

Colleen could only manage to nod and the doctor allowed her to lie back against the pillow.

Jonas looked down at her and unexpectedly felt a knot grow in his throat. "Colleen, how long have you been sick?"

Her eyes latched desperately onto his familiar face. "I...don't know," she murmured weakly. "I went to call the sheep buyer. Then I came back—went to sleep. I don't know."

Helpless tears welled in her eyes. Jonas reached for her hand and squeezed it, trying to reassure both her and himself that she was going to be all right.

While scribbling on his clipboard, the doctor said, "Since you work outdoors and with animals, I'm going to run a blood test just to rule out the possibility of tick fever."

"Will she need to be hospitalized?" Jonas asked quickly.

The doctor shook his head. "If it's bronchitis, hospitalization won't be necessary. Just bed rest and antibiotics. She'll be fine in a few days."

"The fever—" Jonas began worriedly.

"Is very common in a case of acute bronchitis. Don't worry about it. It will go down with medication," the doctor finished. He reached over and patted Jonas on the shoulder. "Let me go instruct the nurse for the blood test. I'll be back in a few minutes."

Jonas nodded and watched the doctor leave the room. The door had just swished closed when he felt a faint tug on his hand. His eyes fell instantly on Colleen and her small hand clinging to his.

"Jonas, my dog—my sheep. I have to go back—"

The worried frown on his face quickly disappeared, and he reached down to brush the hair from her eyes.

"Don't worry about them, Colleen. I brought Dangit with us. And I've already sent one of my hands out to tend the sheep."

Gratitude filled her eyes as she looked up at his concerned face. She didn't know why he was doing this for her, but at the moment she was too weak and sick to wonder about it.

"Thank you, Jonas."

A crooked smile moved his lips as he looked down at her, his fingers continuing to smooth the hair off her forehead. "Don't thank me pretty lady, just get well."

She nodded and in spite of her effort to keep them open, her eyelids fell shut. Moments later she heard the voice of a nurse and felt the sharp jab of a needle in her hip, then another prick in her arm as the person drew blood.

Throughout it all she was aware that Jonas continued to hold her hand. It was a comforting feeling for Colleen. She somehow knew that as long as Jonas was with her, everything would be all right.

Chapter Four

Hours later Colleen opened her eyes to another strange room. It was dark and she was lying in a wide bed with crisp cotton sheets that smelled faintly of lavender. There were two large windows a few feet away from her, but they were both covered with closed venetian blinds.

Blinking her eyes against the semi-darkness, she turned over in the bed and looked at the opposite wall. Moving her body was an effort. She felt as if she'd been beaten and her muscles ached as if she'd climbed several mountains in one day.

There was a faint movement on the floor beside her, and Colleen peered over the side of the bed to see Dangit lying on a braided rug.

"Dangit, my pretty boy?" she whispered weakly to the dog.

The sound of Colleen's voice threw the dog into a joyous fit. Barking, he flopped both front paws onto the bed and attempted to lick her face.

Colleen was doing her best to urge him back off the bed when the door to the room opened. She could see Jonas silhouetted in the light shafting through the door.

"Colleen?"

"Yes. I'm awake," she answered.

He flipped on the overhead light and entered the room. Colleen could see that she was in a bedroom. A very nice bedroom decorated in pinks and blues.

"I heard the dog and thought something must be wrong," he said, his gaze scrutinizing her pale face against the white pillow case. "How are you feeling?"

"Better," she said, pushing against the mattress to bring herself to a sitting position. To her utter dismay she was too weak to do even that and she fell back against the pillow with a helpless sigh.

"Don't try to sit," he said, quickly taking a seat on the edge of the bed and putting a big hand on her shoulder. "Just rest."

"Where am I?" she asked, rubbing her fingers against her eyes. She knew she probably looked as terrible as she felt. It bothered her that Jonas was seeing her in such a condition.

"You're at my house. The doctor said you needed bed rest and care."

Her hands dropped away from her face, but she didn't look up at him. Absently she plucked at the sheet covering her. "I'm not your responsibility."

Jonas studied her face and felt something tighten in his chest. "No," he began slowly, his fingers gently massaging her shoulder. "But I wanted to help."

He wanted to help her. Colleen couldn't understand that. Why would he want to? He knew she couldn't repay him. And she was nothing to him. Nothing at all.

"I—I have friends in Lake City. They—they—" A spurt of coughing interrupted her words. By the time it was over she was out of breath.

Jonas shook his head at her. "You're too weak to be making a trip to Lake City. I have plenty of room. And tomorrow my housekeeper will be here to look after you while I'm at the office. It's no problem having you here, so don't try to pin a medal on me yet," he added with a teasing grin.

In spite of her misgivings she smiled weakly up at him. "I feel terrible about causing you so much trouble."

He looked at her with steady gray eyes. "Feel terrible about having bronchitis, not about me."

Even though she was sick and in a weakened condition, she was suddenly aware that she was alone with this man in a bedroom and he was sitting only inches away from her. "How long have I been asleep?"

Jonas pushed back the cuff of his shirt and glanced at his watch. "I'd say about twelve hours."

"Twelve hours! What time is it?"

"A little after midnight."

"Midnight," she said, aghast. "I'm keeping you up."

He'd never met a woman like her, who worried about everything and everyone except herself. He had the feeling she'd never had anyone to watch out for her, take care of her. She was the one who did the watching out, the caring for, the one who shouldered the responsibility. The idea made Jonas want to protect her even more. But then, he reminded himself, she probably didn't want anyone caring for her.

"Does it look like it's hurt me?" he asked.

Colleen's green eyes slid over him. He looked as manly and handsome as ever, even though his striped shirt was a bit wrinkled and his dark hair had been rumpled by his fingers. "No. I suppose not."

"Good," he said, rising to his feet. "That means I can go get you something to eat. How about chicken soup?"

He was going to cook for her! She couldn't imagine it. "No, you mustn't bother. I'll eat in the morning, when your housekeeper gets here."

Jonas's thick dark brows furrowed in a frown as he looked down at her. "You've gone too long without eating," he said. Not giving her a chance to argue, he turned and started toward the door.

"But—" Colleen began.

With his hand on the doorknob, he glanced back over his shoulder at her. "You're going to quickly learn, Colleen, not to argue with me. I usually get what I want. And right now I want you to eat."

Colleen watched him go out the door, then closed her eyes. A quiet sigh escaped her parted lips. The man didn't understand. He didn't know that she'd been raised to stand on her own. She'd never been beholden to anyone. She didn't know how to accept help.

Minutes later Jonas returned with a tray. On it was a bowl of chicken noodle soup, a glass of juice with crushed ice, and a bottle of medicine.

He placed the tray on a nightstand by the table. Reaching for the pillows beneath Colleen's head, he asked, "Do you think you can sit if I help you?"

She nodded and lifted her head so he could set the pillows against the headboard. With a hand on either side of Colleen's rib cage he virtually lifted her up and back so that she was propped against the pillows.

"I'm really feeling much better," she told him as he set the tray across her lap. "By tomorrow I can go home and—" A spasm of coughing struck her, making the pain in her chest almost unbearable.

Once it passed, Jonas gave her a stern look. "It will be several days before I allow you to go home." He handed her the spoon. "Don't you realize how ill you are?"

Avoiding his gaze she took the spoon and dipped into the soup. "I'm never sick. I suppose I came down with this because I was out in the rain."

Carefully she sipped the warm soup from the spoon. It tasted good and she realized she was ravenously hungry.

"You were in the rain?"

She nodded. “I was caught out with the sheep and didn't have a slicker with me. I was freezing by the time I got back to camp. But I never thought it would make me sick.”

“When was that?” he asked, unable to forget when he'd found her out there on the mountain alone, burning up with fever. He shuddered each time he thought of it.

Her face wrinkled with confusion. “I don't know. Yesterday, maybe?”

Jonas shook his head. “I don't think so. I found you yesterday morning.”

“Oh. I guess I've been out of it longer than I realized,” she said between sips of soup.

It was then she realized she wasn't wearing her own cotton gown. This one was pale pink and silky. Ivory lace edged the capped sleeves and V-neck. It was obviously an expensive garment and she wondered who it belonged to. A girlfriend? His mother? That question was suddenly replaced by how she'd gotten it on. Surely—no, surely Jonas hadn't put it on her, had he?

Color flooded her pale cheeks at the idea of him seeing her body. Jonas saw the red stain on her cheeks and quickly mistook it for fatigue.

“You're getting tired,” he said, his deep voice filled with concern. “Let me have the spoon.”

“No—”

He took the spoon from her and lifted the glass of juice to her lips. “Here, try some of this. You need all the liquids you can drink.”

"What is it?" she asked, trying her best to keep her eyes away from his. There were only inches separating them. Colleen wondered if that space was some sort of magnetic field, for it pulled at her until all she could think of was him.

"Passion fruit," he said with a wry smile.

She took a sip and found it delicious. She'd never tasted passion fruit. Her groceries were limited to the necessary staples. She certainly couldn't afford exotic fruits. But then Jonas was probably already aware of that, she thought.

"I've never tasted it before," she said once she'd taken several sips.

Jonas put the glass down on the tray. "Don't worry, its name is misleading. It's not really an aphrodisiac."

Colleen's blush deepened and she darted a glance up at his dark face as she licked her lips free of the sweet juice. He was smiling at her and she suddenly realized that never in a million years would she have envisioned herself in this position, with Jonas sitting at the edge of her bed, feeding her, teasing her.

Without asking, she knew there wasn't anyone else present in the house. But she didn't feel threatened by the idea. On the contrary, she felt safe, cocooned in his care and his kindness. She also felt like a woman. Albeit a sick woman.

He fed her the remainder of the soup then removed the tray and placed the glass of juice on the nightstand.

The exertion of sitting and eating had drained Colleen, and she welcomed his help as she lay back down in the bed. His hands were gentle as he touched her arm and her shoulder. When he moved one over her forehead it felt cool against her heated flesh.

"You feel feverish," he said. "I want you to take aspirin with your cough syrup."

"I'm not coughing that much," she said as he smoothed the sheet up over her shoulders. She couldn't remember anyone taking such gentle care of her. And who would have thought it of Jonas Dobbs, a big man in or out of the courtroom.

He shook his head slightly as he looked down at her. "Are you always so argumentative? You sound like that damn DA I have to put up with."

She supposed she had been doing a lot of protesting. But she just couldn't turn herself over to him, not even in sickness. He might be showing her the kind, gentle side of him, but he was still a man. That never left Colleen's mind for one second.

"I'm sorry," she murmured.

"No," he said dryly, striding across the bedroom, "you're sick. And for now you're going to let someone else take care of you besides yourself."

He disappeared behind a door and Colleen decided it was a private bathroom. She could hear him rummaging around, but even as she listened to his muffled movements she felt herself already growing sleepy again.

"Colleen, don't go to sleep yet. Here's the aspirin."

Her eyes opened to see he was back at the bedside. He gave her the tablets and a drink of the juice. After he'd poured a spoonful of the cough syrup he said, "This is the last of the medicine for today."

She looked at him in surprise. She didn't remember taking any other medicine. "You mean you gave me medicine earlier today? I don't remember. How did you do it?"

Laughter rumbled from deep within his chest. "Believe me, Colleen, I did it with much difficulty. You're a terrible patient."

She swallowed the bitter cough syrup and closed her eyes. Her chest hurt and she was very tired. Too tired to stay awake and talk to him. "You must be a good doctor, Jonas," she murmured sleepily.

He smiled and leaned over her. Colleen could feel his nearness. The warmth of his breath touched her cheek a second before his lips did.

"Good night, Colleen," he said softly. "The door will be open. If you need me just call. I'll be right across the hall."

He would be near. If she needed him he would be near. It was the last thought in Colleen's mind before sleep claimed her.

The next morning the housekeeper found Colleen out of bed, searching for her clothes.

"Miss McNair! You shouldn't be out of bed!"

Colleen looked up to see a short plump woman with salt-and-pepper hair, hands planted on either side of her hips.

"I have to get dressed and go," Colleen said in a rush. "There're things I must see to."

"I'm Rose, the housekeeper," the woman introduced herself. "Jonas says you have a bad case of bronchitis and that you're supposed to stay in bed."

Colleen started to dispute her words but a spate of coughing prevented it. "Jonas—doesn't understand," she finally managed to say. "Do you know where my clothes are?"

Rose bustled farther into the room and reached for a phone on the nightstand. "If you don't go back to bed I'm calling him right now."

"I can't go back to bed! Please, I want my clothes."

With a grim expression Rose punched out the number of Jonas's law office. In a matter of moments she was speaking to him. "She's out of bed, Jonas. Yes, I did. It didn't help. Yes, just a moment."

Rose thrust the phone out to Colleen. Colleen automatically stepped back as if the phone was suddenly going to materialize into Jonas himself.

"He wants to speak with you," Rose said.

Seeing no way to avoid it, Colleen took the receiver.

"Hello."

"Colleen, what are you doing? Trying to give poor Rose a bad time?"

His deep familiar voice pulled at something inside her and she suddenly remembered that he'd kissed her on the cheek. Which was a bad thing to be remembering. It made her thinking process completely haywire. "No. But Jonas—"

"Then go back to bed before you give yourself a relapse," he said in a voice that brooked no argument.

Frustration swept over her. "Jonas, you don't understand. The sheep buyer will be out to get the sheep and I must—"

"The sheep buyer has already come and gone," he said, "so quit worrying about him."

"Wh-what?" she stuttered with shock.

Jonas let out a long sigh. He hadn't wanted to give Colleen this news so early in the day. He'd wanted her to be feeling better. But it looked as though the choice had been taken from him. "The sheep buyer came out to your camp yesterday. I had Virgil pay him for his trouble and send him on his way."

"You what!" she practically shouted. Her legs began to tremble and she was forced to sit down on the edge of the bed before she collapsed on the floor.

"I sent him back to Grand Junction and paid him for his trip."

"But the sheep! I have to sell them! The money—I have to have it by tomorrow and—"

"Forget about the mortgages right now. I talked to the officers at the bank and explained that you were ill. They've conceded to give you a few more days."

For long moments Colleen sat without moving or speaking.

"Did you hear me, Colleen? You can quit worrying about it. Your sheep are still on the mountain. Virgil is watching over them, and for the time being your land is safe from any purchasers."

Colleen felt herself begin to shake from head to toe, and it wasn't from weakness. She was suddenly filled with a strange mixture of emotions. Fear, dread, anger and relief. They were all boiling inside her until she felt the only thing left to do was burst into tears.

"Yes, I heard you," she said huskily, then leaned over and dropped the receiver back into its cradle.

She'd barely sunk back against the pillows before the phone began to ring again. Rose picked it up.

"Yes," the woman answered. "Yes, she's in bed now." She darted a concerned look over at Colleen then lowered the receiver and covered it with her hand.

"He wants to talk to you again," she said.

Colleen shook her head. She was in too much of a turmoil to talk to him again. Tears were already beginning to roll down her cheeks.

"She doesn't want to talk, Jonas. I think you should let her rest now. Yes, of course. I'll see that she eats and takes her medicine. Yes, I'll look for you then."

Rose put down the phone and looked at Colleen's miserable expression.

"Honey, I don't know what you and Jonas were just discussing, but whatever it is, it can't be that bad."

Colleen wiped her eyes and looked at the housekeeper. "He's a bully," she sniffed.

Rose looked flabbergasted. "Jonas? A bully? Why, he's one of the kindest men I know."

A fresh wall of tears filled Colleen's eyes. Maybe he was to Rose, and his family and friends. But she didn't fit into any of those categories. She was just a woman in a helpless position and Jonas was taking advantage of the fact. "He's taken over my life. When—I specifically asked him not to!"

Rose smiled with gentle understanding. "Well, I'm sure once you're feeling better you'll get it back."

"Get what back?" Colleen asked as her mind whirled with the problem of finding another sheep buyer and getting the sheep sold and paid for by next week.

"Your life," Rose answered. "You said he'd taken it over."

"Oh," she said, doing her best to turn her thoughts back to the housekeeper. "Yes, he has, but I fully intend to change that."

Rose clucked her tongue and began to straighten the sheet over Colleen. "Why don't you forget all about Jonas right now. I'll fix you a nice breakfast and then with my help you can take a quick shower. Maybe by this evening you'll feel more like facing Jonas, and let him have it with both barrels."

Sighing, Colleen looked at Rose more closely. The woman had a sweet, pretty face. She was about the age Colleen's mother would have been if she'd lived. "You're very nice, Rose. My name is Colleen, by the way. Colleen McNair."

Rose smiled knowingly as she moved toward the door. "Yes, I know. Jonas has told me all about you."

The housekeeper disappeared into the hall, leaving Colleen lying there with a stunned expression on her face.

Colleen ate a breakfast of toast, scrambled eggs and juice. After a quick shower, Rose helped her dress in another clean gown. It was soft yellow with spaghetti straps and a matching bed jacket.

"Who does this belong to?" Colleen asked the housekeeper.

Rose pulled back the sheet and helped Colleen into bed. "Jonas's mother, Juanita."

His mother wore sexy garments like this? "It's very beautiful," Colleen murmured while fingering the delicate fabric.

"I can't imagine Juanita wearing anything that wasn't pretty or glamorous. Have you ever seen her?"

Colleen shook her head.

"She's a very beautiful woman. Her mother was a Mexican lady and Juanita inherited her black hair and café au lait complexion. But that's not really what makes her so beautiful. She has a heart big enough for three people. She's always helping others. In fact, she's in Grand Junction right now helping with a summer program for underprivileged children.

"And don't worry about the gowns. Juanita would be put out if you didn't wear them."

Colleen looked down at herself in the yellow garment. It was unlike anything she'd ever worn, but then, she'd never been in a situation such as this, either.

Colleen wondered if Jonas was like his mother. Maybe he had a thing for strays in need. It was the only logical reason she could think of for his wanting to help her. It bothered Colleen to think he saw her as a pathetic case. She wasn't pathetic, she told herself, she was just a victim of circumstance. But she intended to change that. Somehow, someway, she would get out of this mess. She'd pay the loans her father had taken on and be independent and self-sufficient again.

"Juanita sounds like a lovely woman," Colleen murmured as Rose straightened the bed covers.

"I'm sure you'll meet her before you leave the Slash D, and then you can see for yourself." With a reassuring smile, Rose started toward the door. "Right now I'm going to let you sleep. Nothing better for a sick body."

Rose vanished behind the bedroom door and Colleen let out a long sigh. Now that the housekeeper was out of sight she realized just how exhausted eating and showering had made her.

Closing her eyes she tried to concentrate on making plans of what to do once she was back home. But her mind refused to work and it was only moments before she was sound asleep.

Late that afternoon Colleen woke to the muffled sound of footsteps next to her bed. Opening her eyes, she turned over to see Jonas standing over her, a glass of juice in one hand, a bottle of medicine in the other.

"Hello, Colleen. How are you feeling?"

The past few hours he'd been away had almost made her forget how big and good-looking he was. She stared up at his dark face trying to remember all the things she'd been planning to say to him, but none of them came to mind.

"Better, thank you," she said, her voice still husky with sleep.

He handed the glass of juice to her then shook out a capsule from the medicine bottle. "You're looking much better. Have you been coughing?"

"Only a little. The medicine must be doing its work." She swallowed the capsule and Jonas placed the glass on the nightstand.

"Rose tells me you ate breakfast and lunch."

"I didn't want to disappoint her. She went to a lot of trouble."

Frowning, Jonas sat down on the side of the bed. As if he had that right without so much as asking, Colleen thought.

"Damn it, Colleen, that's no reason to eat! You should eat because you're hungry!"

His words stung her, making her green eyes widen. "Maybe I should ask you why you always have to be the person in charge," she retorted. "I told you in simple English that I'd take care of my own business. But you went right ahead and took matters into your own hands. Now I'm going to have to find another sheep buyer."

"I kept you from making a terrible mistake," he pointed out. "Most people would be thanking me."

"I'm not most people."

So he'd discovered, Jonas thought. She was unlike any woman he'd known, except for one. And he didn't want to be reminded of that mistake. "It's not as painful to accept help as you might think. All you have to do is try it."

"I'm very angry with you," she said, ignoring his words.

His brows arched innocently while a crooked smile gave her a glimpse of his white teeth. It was obvious that he didn't take her anger seriously. "You are?" he asked.

Colleen heaved out a frustrated sigh. "Yes, I am. Is that so hard to understand? Would you like someone taking over your personal business?"

He chuckled. "The DA tries to take over my business all the time."

"Bull!" she snapped, rising earnestly up on one elbow.

"No, the subject is sheep, not bull," he said dryly.

Colleen's head swung helplessly back and forth. It was beyond her to know how to reason with this man.

"Jonas, you're deliberately—"

His hand reached over and closed around her upper arm. The action so surprised Colleen that her words halted in midsentence.

"You called me Jonas when you were out of your head with fever, but you're not feverish now. Things are definitely getting better between us."

Getting better between them? What was he talking about? It was impossible to think when he touched her. He was so close that with each breath she took she drew in the scent of him. Her eyes could see the coarse texture of his dark hair and skin, the lines at the corner of his gray eyes, the thick black lashes, the faint shadow of beard, the sensual curve of his lips. Her eyes clung to the last feature as his fingers on her arm caused a heat to spread all the way up her shoulder and into her face.

"It was a slip of the tongue," she finally managed to say.

"I hope it does a lot more slipping," he said.

Jonas watched her eyes lower from his and a blush color her cheeks. It dawned on him that Colleen wasn't used to being touched or teased or any of the things most women her age would consider second nature. He wanted to change all that. But he knew that to do that he'd have to get close to her, and that was something he couldn't let himself do.

Jonas's fingers moved ever so slightly up and down her arm, then pulled away. Colleen went limp with relief. If he'd kept touching her, she didn't know what she might have ended up saying or doing.

"The bank," she spoke up. "How long did they agree to give me?"

He frowned, but Colleen didn't see it. Her eyes were on his arms and hands. He'd rolled back the sleeves of his brown pin-striped shirt to reveal thick corded muscles, the tops of which were furred with black hair. A gold watch encircled his left wrist. The face of it was black and she knew from the sleek shape and design that it was an expensive piece of jewelry. Or at least it would be to her. To Jonas it had probably been peanuts.

"I told them we'd be in next week, after you were feeling better."

Colleen's head jerked up. "We? There's not going to be any 'we' about it. I'm going to find another sheep buyer."

Jonas was amazed at how much her distrust hurt. He'd been distrusted before, but that had been by criminals behind bars, guilty people who were angry at him because he'd refused to take their cases. But having a woman such as Colleen attack his morality wounded him more than he cared to admit. "You still don't trust me, do you? Somewhere in that head of yours you think I'm trying to con you, don't you?" he asked, his gray eyes piercing hers.

"I don't know what to think," she whispered hoarsely.

The confusion and uncertainty on her face took away some of Jonas's anger. She was so alone in the world and afraid that he was going to hurt her, take advantage of her. He knew she needed reassurance, but then so did he. He wished he had his own assurance that this whole thing wasn't going to backfire in his face.

Sighing, Jonas raked his fingers through his hair. "Look, Colleen, I have no intention of taking your land from you. My Lord, I have plenty of my own. What would I want with it?"

"Maybe for the same reason Roger does," she said sharply.

Jonas cursed under his breath.

Colleen was suddenly exhausted and she fell back against the pillows. Earlier she'd put on the bed jacket in case Jonas might walk in unexpectedly. She was thankful that she had, and now she unconsciously pulled the front of it even closer together, as if by doing so she could shut Jonas out of her life.

"I don't know why you had to interfere in the first place," she told him. "I could have sold the sheep, gotten myself out of debt, and it would all be over by now."

His expression was suddenly dry. "You're pretty damn ungrateful, aren't you?"

"Ungrateful!" she gasped. "Why you—"

"You were delirious," he cut in quickly, "when I found you out there on the mountain. If it hadn't been for me—"

"I didn't ask you to help me!" she angrily interrupted his words. "I didn't ask you to send the sheep buyer away! I didn't ask you to plead my excuses with the bank!"

"Why can't you just see this as one person helping another?" he asked her angrily.

If it had been anyone other person than Jonas, she probably could have. "Because it's like you said in the car lot that day. Everybody wants something for nothing, even you, Jonas."

A blank look came over his face and Colleen watched him rise from the bed and walk over to the window. He opened the blinds and for long minutes studied the mountains and valleys in the far distance.

For days now, Jonas had carried an idea around in his head. It had plagued his every waking moment, and even now he wasn't quite sure whether his idea was either completely insane or the most brilliant legal maneuver he'd yet to come up with. "You know, Colleen," he ventured, hoping his voice sounded more steady than he felt, "you and I are a lot alike."

She stared at him. "How could you possibly say that? We're nothing alike. We have nothing in common."

He turned his head slightly to toss her a mocking smile over his shoulder. "You're wrong about that. We both have common needs."

Needs? Colleen couldn't imagine Jonas needing anything. He had a beautiful home, a prosperous ranch, a successful career. "I think you have one of us mixed up with somebody else," she said.

He moved away from the window and back to the bed, this time taking a seat at the foot of it. Colleen continued to hold the bed jacket securely against her breast.

"No, I don't think so," he said, his face suddenly very serious as he watched her closely.

Colleen had the distinct feeling he was silently testing her, weighing her. She didn't like the feeling at all. "It's obvious I need money—I still do if I'm ever going to free my land of mortgagers. But I can't see where you need—"

Her words ceased abruptly as his hand came up in a gesture for her to halt.

"What do you think I need, Colleen?"

She didn't know why he was asking her such a question, but she made a point of answering honestly. She looked at him, then allowed her eyes to travel over the opulent fixtures of the room. "I can't imagine you needing anything. You don't appear to me to be a man that's lacking."

Jonas had never thought of himself as lacking, at least not materially. But there were those who thought he was lacking in other ways. "Colleen, I know how much you love your land. I've seen how valiantly you are willing to fight for it. So maybe you can understand when I tell you that I love my land just as passionately. And I'm just as willing to do things out of the ordinary to hang on to mine."

Colleen forgot all about the bed jacket as she raised up from the pillows. "What are you trying to tell me, Jonas? That you want my land after all?"

His gray eyes held on to hers for long moments, searching, questioning. The tenseness of his features relayed itself to Colleen. She gripped the sheet as she waited for him to answer.

"No, I want a wife."

Chapter Five

Colleen stared at him as if he'd lost his mind. "A wife? Is this your idea of a crude joke?"

Frowning, he rose from the bed and began to move restlessly around the room. "A joke is supposed to be something funny, Colleen. There's nothing funny about this."

"Well, I'm afraid I find it deliriously funny. You need a wife? There's probably dozens of women in Gunnison who'd want to marry you. All you have to do is take your pick. I can't see where that would be a problem for any man unless he was bashful, and you're certainly not that."

Any other time Jonas would have laughed, but at the moment he couldn't rouse himself enough to find anything amusing. "It is a problem when you don't want a wife for the usual reasons," he said.

"What do you mean, 'usual reasons'?" Colleen asked warily.

He stood at the foot of the bed again, his hands curved around one of the fat cornerposts. Colleen looked so lovely lying there in his bed, his house, and he thought of how soft her skin had felt when he'd helped her before. His voice was soft as he answered, thinking about the few times he'd touched her. "You know. Love, children, that sort of thing."

Yes, Colleen did know. A few years ago those were the reasons why she'd wanted to marry. Those were also the two reasons she'd been hurt so badly when it had failed to happen. "Then I can't imagine why you would want to marry if it weren't for those reasons."

Jonas turned his gaze in the direction of the windows. "Because my mother wants me to."

Colleen laughed with disbelief. "And you always do what your mother wants? Frankly, you look all grown up to me. Why don't you just tell her no?"

Jonas made an impatient sound then came back around the bed to take a seat on the edge of the mattress. "It's not that simple, Colleen. I have told her no. Actually, that's what got me into this mess in the first place. I kept telling her and Dad I had no intention or desire to marry. They wanted me to have a wife and family." He stopped and shrugged as though the whole thing had been taken out of his hands. "So before my father died he revised his will saying if I wasn't married by my thirty-fifth birthday the ranch was to be sold and the sum given to my mother."

Colleen couldn't believe what she was hearing. "That's ludicrous! Why would they do something like that?"

Sighing heavily, Jonas looked away from her. "The why isn't important. The fact is if I'm not married within the year the Slash D will no longer be mine. So you see, I know exactly how you're feeling. That's why I thought we could work together on this."

Her green eyes took on a dazed look. "Work together? How?"

There was something strange about the expression on his face. Colleen felt herself growing cold as she waited for him to answer.

"You need money. I need a wife. We can help each other."

Colleen literally reared backward at his words, as though putting distance between them could somehow protect her from his suggestion. "You—you're insane! I don't want to marry anyone—much less you!"

"That's good. We won't have to worry about where we stand with each other. It will be purely a business arrangement."

What he was asking of her was the coldest, most unfeeling thing she'd ever heard. Suddenly everything about the whole situation began to sink in. Pain and humiliation rushed at her from every direction. Everything he'd done for her had been to set her up for this!

Before Jonas knew her intentions she was tossing back the covers and scrambling out of the bed. "Colleen—"

"Get my clothes! I want out of here!"

Jonas started across the room to her only to have her back away from him, a wild light in her eyes.

"Colleen, you're ill. Get back in bed."

"I'm sick all right. Sick to think you might have actually wanted to help me," she spat at him.

He lifted his hand in a defensive gesture. "I am trying to help you," he said in a patient voice. "What's so wrong about me wanting your help in return?"

"I think you're despicable. No wonder you and Roger are friends, you're exactly alike!"

Jonas didn't know what that was supposed to mean, but at the moment it didn't matter. He was more concerned about getting her back to bed. "Colleen, you're becoming hysterical. Please get back in bed. We'll talk about this later."

Colleen felt she couldn't endure another minute in this man's house, much less his bed. "I'm going home. Now!"

"You can't. You're not well enough to stand, much less go home."

He started toward her, and Colleen's heart began to flutter rapidly. Feeling utterly trapped and desperate, her eyes darted around the room for the best route of escape.

"Colleen, please—"

Before he could say anything else she rushed past him, toward the door. Jonas caught her before she reached it, his arms clamping around her slender body.

Colleen began to struggle wildly. "Let me go! I want—" Her words were cut off by a violent spate of coughing.

"Colleen, my God, you're going to lose your breath!" Frightened by the spasms racking her, Jonas bent down and scooped her up in his arms.

She felt light as a feather, and beneath the sheer material of the gown her flesh felt too warm. "Crazy woman! Are you trying to kill yourself?"

She was still coughing when he lay her gently on the bed, but it began to ebb away as he covered her up. Jonas tucked the blanket around her shoulders, then reached up and brushed the soft fringe of bangs from her forehead.

"I'm sorry, Colleen," he whispered. "Lie back and go to sleep. Forget I ever mentioned any of this. It was a crazy idea anyway."

The tenderness in his voice touched Colleen in a place she'd long tried to keep hidden. With resigned defeat, she closed her eyes and allowed her muscles to go limp against the mattress. "Just leave me alone, Jonas," she mumbled miserably.

He didn't say anything, and after a few moments Colleen felt him move away from her and leave the room.

Colleen tried her best to sleep, but all she could manage to do was stare into the darkness of the bedroom while her mind dwelled on one word. Wife. Jonas wanted her to be his wife. Not because he loved her but because he loved his land.

For some illogical reason that hurt. Deep down she'd wanted to believe that Jonas had started out helping her because he'd cared about her. But it hadn't been that way. All along he'd had a more selfish, ulterior motive.

But men were selfish creatures—she'd learned that the hard way. She'd also vowed never to love one, trust one, or marry one. And just because Jonas had put this proposition to her didn't mean she had to accept it.

She had another option. She could still sell the sheep. *But where would that leave you?* a tiny voice inside her asked. With a piece of land with nothing on it? What would she do then? How could she start over? What would she live on? But on the other hand, what would she have if she married Jonas?

The questions continued to plague her until some two hours later, when Jonas returned to her room with a tray of food.

She was surprised to see him. She hadn't expected him to come to her room again tonight.

"Do you think you can eat now?" he asked, switching on a lamp by the bedside.

Colleen's eyes traveled over him as he placed the tray on the nightstand. He'd changed his slacks and shirt for a pair of jeans and a black T-shirt. He looked young and virile and sexy. She wondered who the real man was beneath the tough exterior: a shrewd lawyer, a businessman willing to go to extra lengths to keep his ranch or the compassionate man she'd hoped he'd been?

As she looked at him she realized that time alone in the darkened bedroom had allowed some of the initial shock and outrage at him to wear off. To turn down supper just to spite him would be foolish on her part. "Yes, I think so," she told him.

Nodding, he waited for her to smooth the blankets across her lap to make a place for the tray.

"Rose made a casserole with beef and noodles. And there's apple cake for dessert."

Self-consciously Colleen pushed her fingers through her hair. She knew she probably looked awful, but then Jonas wasn't interested in her looks, he was only interested in what she could legally do for him. It was a sobering thought.

"I'm sure I'll enjoy it," she told him, deliberately keeping her eyes on the food and away from his face.

"If you need anything else just call out. I'll be right down the hall."

He turned to go. Surprise lifted her eyes to his back. She hadn't expected him to leave so quickly and she realized she was disappointed to see him go. The feeling didn't make sense, but then not much had made sense to Colleen since Jonas first walked into her camp.

"Jonas?"

Colleen could feel him turning slowly back to her and her heart began to thud heavily.

"Yes," he answered.

"I—" She picked up her fork, then lifted her eyes up to his. "If we—if we did get married—what would I get out of the deal?"

He folded his big arms across his chest as he stood looking down at her, his expression carefully controlled. "Your mortgages would be paid, your land would be debt-free. This house would be your home, and, of course, as your husband, I would be responsible for your financial security."

Her husband. Just the idea of it made Colleen quake inside. "And how long would this arrangement last?"

The look on his face said he found her question odd. "Just like any other marriage, 'til death do us part'."

"Are you mad?" she gasped.

"Not since I last checked."

"But—but what if you—you might fall in love with someone and then I'd be in the way."

His face was suddenly guarded. "The same could be said of you."

Colleen made a disgusted sound as she looked back down at the tray on her lap. "That would never happen. I'm not the least bit interested in falling in love."

Neither was he. After Lana, Jonas had steered clear of serious relationships with women. It was safer that way. But he wondered why Colleen seemed so determined to avoid men, marriage and love. "I'm not either," he said, "so that takes care of that problem."

Colleen deliberately made herself dig into the food on her plate, but even as she ate, her mind was whirling. She'd always thought she was a strong, determined woman. She'd always believed that avoiding love and marriage was a sound decision where her future was concerned. But now, hearing the words spoken aloud, it all sounded so cold, so final.

Jonas sat down in the rocker beside the bed and looked at her questioningly. "Are you trying to tell me you're considering my proposal after all?"

Funny that he should call it a proposal. A proposal was usually associated with rings and kisses and vows of love. Yet this one was filled with doubts, suspicions and legal realities. Well, the first kind hadn't worked for her, she thought sadly. Did that mean this kind would? "Marrying you is the last thing I want to do."

Jonas's eyes traveled over her closely as, bite after bite, she brought the food to her mouth. What would it be like, he wondered, to have her living in the house with him, as his wife? Would it change her, change him?

"What's the first?" he asked.

To be out of this house, she thought, and away from Jonas. Yet even so, she'd learned over the past weeks that being away from Jonas didn't necessarily mean he was out of her thoughts. "To secure my land."

"That's my most important want, too," Jonas assured her.

Colleen slanted him a sidelong glance. "Why haven't you married someone else before now?"

One of his shoulders lifted and fell as though he considered her question insignificant. "I was engaged to be married once. It didn't work out."

Colleen suddenly forgot her food. Something in his voice gave her the impression that he was being deliberately nonchalant. She wondered what kind of woman he'd been involved with. "Why didn't things work out? What happened?"

His mouth a tight line, he leaned back in the rocker, making the runners creak from the tilted position. The sound was loud in the quiet bedroom, reminding Colleen how alone they were in the house. How would it be if they were married, she wondered. He'd said it would be purely a business arrangement. She supposed that meant at best they would be friends. Nothing more. The idea should have been consoling, but it wasn't.

"I met Lana in college," he said, his voice deliberately flat, emotionless. "She was beautiful and a brilliant law student. I was captivated by her. And for a while I thought she was by me."

"For a while?"

His eyes fell away from Colleen. "Until it was time for her to choose between our marriage or her career."

Colleen was surprised. "Can you blame her? After all, she studied and worked the same as you for her degree."

Frowning, Jonas got to his feet and began to move restlessly around the room. Colleen's eyes followed him.

"I wasn't asking her to give it up," he said after a moment. "The fact was when it came right down to it, Lana didn't want to be a wife. She was independent, she didn't need a full-time man in her life. All she needed or wanted was a courtroom."

Colleen put down her fork, then leaned over and set the tray on the nightstand. "Then you should be thankful she chose it instead of you."

He stopped pacing long enough to look at her, one brow arching wryly. "Oh?"

Colleen lifted her chin a fraction. "You don't look like a man who'd like to be second in anything."

She was right, he thought, a bit surprised that she had noticed such things about him. He wasn't a man who was content to play second fiddle. Maybe that was why he'd been so scarred when Lana had pushed him aside for a life of her own. "Well, this thing with you and me—it allows both of us to be winners."

Colleen couldn't imagine it. No more than she could imagine living the rest of her life with this man. "People would think we were crazy. We hardly know each other." She could already hear what his acquaintances would say. Jonas must be getting hard up after all, he's gone and plucked a little lost lamb off the mountain.

Shaking her head, Colleen said, "'Til death do us part might be a long time."

"Would that be so bad?" he asked. "You'd have a good home here. From what you've told me before you don't want to have children."

Everything he was saying was true, but something inside of her rose up to rebel against it, and she didn't know why. "That's right. But what about you? Wouldn't you like children of your own? A son to carry on your name?"

At one time in his life Jonas had wanted children very much. But after Lana he hadn't allowed himself to dream or want those kind of things. He couldn't allow himself to do it now, because it was more than obvious to him that Colleen was the same sort of woman that Lana had been. In one way that made her safe, but on the other hand it also made her very dangerous.

"My ranch is what I want," he said brusquely, putting distance between them. "I thought you would understand that. None of this has anything to do with love, or children, candlelight or roses."

Colleen couldn't help it; she felt wounded by his words. But to let him know that would be like admitting that she cared about him. And she didn't. She never would, she fiercely told herself. "That's exactly what I want to make sure of," she said sharply.

"You can be damn sure of it. I'm not in the market for romance."

Suddenly weary, she said, "So I guess things are black-and-white now. You want to keep your land, I want to keep mine. I guess you were right after all, we do have something in common."

There was bleak resignation in the tone of her voice. What had he expected her to do? To sound like? As if she were madly in love with him? As if she wanted more than anything to be his wife?

"Does this mean you're saying yes?" he asked.

She closed her eyes, blotting out the sight of him standing there beside the bed. "I'm considering it, that's all. Now if you don't mind, I'm very tired. I'd like to go to sleep."

Jonas studied her for a long time, taking in her face with its smooth skin, full lips, and thick brown lashes resting against angular cheekbones. She looked very fragile, very vulnerable, and Jonas was suddenly compelled to lean down and pull the covers up over her shoulders, smooth the hair back from her brow. He didn't want to hurt her, far from it. But he didn't want to fall in love with her, either. He felt as if he were walking a thin, dangerous line.

At the soft touch of his fingers Colleen's eyes fluttered open and she found herself looking straight into Jonas's gray eyes.

"I don't want you to worry, Colleen. Whatever you might think of me, I'd never do anything to hurt you."

Colleen desperately wanted to believe him. Because at this very moment she had the feeling her future hinged upon this man. "I guess I'll find that out soon enough."

Jonas had the sudden longing to lean down and kiss her, to try to assure her with his lips where his words had so far failed. But kissing wasn't a part of business deals and that was what theirs had to be. "Yes, I guess you will," he said, trying to keep the frustration from his voice.

Reaching over he picked up the dirty tray and switched off the lamp. "Good night, Colleen."

"Good night, Jonas, and thank you for bringing my supper."

He glanced at her, amazed that one minute she could be fighting him so and the next minute thanking him. "I'd like to think you'd do the same for me."

Yes, she would do as much for him, she realized. The difference was Colleen would be doing it just for him, not because she wanted something from him. But it wasn't important that he should know that. Theirs was to be an impersonal relationship. "I wouldn't let a sick lamb tend to himself. Not even you."

So now she was comparing him to one of her lambs, he thought, finding the idea oddly pleasing. If there was one thing Colleen did care about, it was her lambs. With a faint smile on his face, Jonas turned and quietly left the room.

Colleen was awake early the next morning, half-expecting Jonas to come to her room and demand an answer to his proposal before he left for his law office. But by the time Rose showed up with her breakfast tray, she decided he'd already left the house.

Through the open blinds she could see the sun streaming down over the tops of the mountains, flowing down into the cracks and crevices like golden lava. The beauty of it and the fact that she was feeling much stronger lifted Colleen's spirits and she smiled warmly at the housekeeper. "Rose, I'd really like to get out of bed today. Do you think you could find my clothes?"

"Well, now," she said, thoughtfully tapping a finger against her chin. "I can't remember Jonas showing me any of your things. The only clothing of yours I've seen around here is the nightgown he brought you home in."

Colleen picked up a hot muffin from the tray, broke it open and quickly spread the two sides with butter. "I suppose he didn't think to get any from my tent," she mused aloud, then glanced back up to Rose. "What about my dog, Dangit? He was here in the house when I first woke, but I haven't seen him since."

"He's fine," Rose hastened to assure her. "He's made pals with a couple of the ranch dogs, and he's being fed regularly."

Colleen smiled to herself. "I guess he's seeing this whole thing as a vacation. I can't ever remember a time he's been away from the flock."

Rose pulled up the rocker Jonas had sat in the previous night, took a seat and crossed her thick ankles out in front of her. "Jonas tells me you run a flock of sheep all by yourself. I just can't imagine that."

Colleen nodded proudly. Raising sheep was the one thing she felt confident about. "I've done it all my life. It's not that hard, until lambing season, and then you have to watch the ewes almost constantly. Many of them have trouble lambing and need help."

"And where did you learn about sheep, from your folks?"

"From my father," Colleen said after swallowing a bite of the muffin. "He raised them all his life, right on the very spot my sheep are on now."

Rose smiled knowingly at the pride in Colleen's voice. "That's the way it is with Jonas. His father ran cattle on this land for nearly forty years, and his grandfather fifty before that. Now there was a man who saw some changes in his time. Indians, miners, trappers, ranchers and farmers. He lived among them all."

"Is Jonas very involved with running the Slash D?" Colleen asked casually.

Rose rolled her eyes. "Good Lord, the man thinks he has to oversee every sack of grain and every bale of hay that comes onto this place. Not one calf or cow is sold unless Jonas has looked at it and made the final decision. No bull goes near the herd unless Jonas is there to oversee it. Sometimes I think he works too hard here on the ranch. Especially when he has his law practice, too."

So he was dedicated to the place, Colleen thought. At least what he'd told her had been the truth. "Well, when land has been handed down from generation to generation, it usually holds a place in a person's heart. It's probably important for Jonas to see it flourish."

"Too important," Rose said with a frown, then got to her feet and straightened the apron covering her red shirtwaister. "Now if Jonas put as much love and attention toward a woman as he does into this ranch, he'd be far better off in my opinion. Juanita's too. But I'm rattling now, and wasting time," she said with a sigh. "Can I get you anything else before I go?"

Colleen looked down at the laden tray, then shook her head. "No. Unless you could find something for me to wear after I finish my breakfast?"

Rose pulled the dust rag from her shoulder and started out the door. "I'll find something," she promised.

Almost an hour later, Rose returned with a pair of blue jeans and a white shirt. To Colleen's surprise the jeans were only a size bigger than her own and the shirt fit her almost perfectly. "Where did you get these?"

"They fit pretty good, if I say so myself," Rose said, obviously pleased with herself. "They belong to Jonas's mother. She keeps jeans and things out here so she can ride whenever the whim hits her. There's a pair of boots in the closet, too, but I'm not going to give them to you today. You might be tempted to go outside."

"So you're just going to leave me barefooted?" Colleen asked with dismay.

Rose cackled with laughter. "That's better than having Jonas after me. He thinks I'm going to keep you in bed again all day."

The smile on Colleen's face was instantly replaced by grim determination. She desperately resented the idea that Jonas thought he had her in the palm of his hand. "If he thinks he's going to boss me around, he's got another think coming. I'm my own boss."

In spite of her anxiousness to be on her feet, Colleen discovered she was still too weak to stay up for very long periods. After lunch she slept and eventually woke up in time to go out to the kitchen to watch Rose prepare the evening meal.

Colleen would have liked to help with the cooking, but the housekeeper was adamant, insisting that she sit on a stepchair and nothing more.

The kitchen was a long room, the cabinets and fixtures done in sparkling white. A row of windows faced the west. From where Colleen sat she could see far into a shallow valley. It was dotted with red cattle grazing in the waning afternoon light. It was a beautiful view, just one of many that could be seen from the Slash D ranch house. It was no wonder that Jonas loved this place, that he was even willing to take on a wife to keep it. The question was, did Colleen want to hang on to her own place badly enough to marry him?

"Do you have a boyfriend, Colleen?" Rose asked, as she scrubbed carrots beneath a stream of cold tap water.

Unable to avoid the question, Colleen answered as noncommittally as she could. "No, I don't. I really don't have time for one."

Rose clucked her tongue. "Just like Jonas. That's the saddest thing I've ever heard of. I can't imagine life without my husband or my kids. Course that's not to say that having a family is always a bed of roses. Families are work." She looked over her shoulder, cocking one thin brow in Colleen's direction. "But then on the other side of the fence, it's nice to have someone around to remind you that you're loved. I've always thought that's what living was all about." Shrugging, she turned back to the sink.

"But I admit that things are different these days. Women are different. Lots of them don't want to be tied down to a man. They like their independence. But I just wonder how they'll feel about that once they get old. And if we live, we all get old. There isn't any way to get around it."

Rose's philosophy was something to think about, and for a moment Colleen tried to look into her own future. What would it be like if she didn't marry Jonas? Empty, alone? What would it be like if she did? Would he even care enough to be her companion, or would she just be someone who happened to live and sleep under the same roof?

Chapter Six

The meal was in the oven keeping warm and Rose had already left by the time Jonas arrived home. The house was hushed as he stepped inside, and Jonas quietly hung up his hat and headed for the den, trying not to disturb Colleen if she was sleeping. He was just about to enter the room when he saw her, and he stopped in the doorway, barely breathing, watching her.

She was standing by the tall windows, her face wistful as she gazed out over the yard. Her arms were hugging her waist as if, even when she was alone, she felt the need to protect herself. Her strawberry-blond hair had been brushed to a shiny halo around her face, and beneath the hems of the jeans her feet were bare. There was an odd mixture of grace and vulnerableness as she stood so completely unaware of him, and

Jonas realized he'd never seen a woman more beautiful to him than she was at that moment.

"Colleen, should you be up?" he asked gently.

She turned sharply at the sound of his voice to see him stepping down into the den. The sight of him never failed to stir her, and it did so even more now because she had been thinking of him, wondering about the answer she'd decided to give him. "I'm feeling much stronger, and I couldn't bear being in bed for another moment."

He closed the distance between them even as he made a quick assessment of her. There was a healthy pink color back in her cheeks, and she looked rested for the first time in days. He'd been worried that she wouldn't recover, had lain awake at night thinking that she could have died on that mountain if he hadn't decided to drive out to see her. Sometimes he wondered if a part of him wanted to marry her just so he could rest assured that she would never be alone and hurt again.

"I had a late appointment with a client," he explained, trying to ignore the soft thoughts. "Is our supper ruined?"

Colleen shook her head. "Rose put it in the oven before she left."

"If you're ready to eat, I'll go wash."

She nodded, and Jonas turned and left the room. Colleen followed, slowly making her way down the hallway to the dining room where Rose had already set the table.

It was a formal room with heavily draped windows and a delicate white-and-gold printed wallpaper covering the walls. Two stained-glass lamps hung over the long polished oak table. Along one wall was a matching antique buffet, and cornered next to it was a glass hutch of the same design. Thick winter-white carpet sank beneath Colleen's feet as she walked over to the buffet to examine a pitcher and bowl set.

In spite of the room's formality, there was still a ranch house style to it, with the wooden beams supporting the ceiling and the distinct taste of the furniture and decorations. Colleen loved the room, as she was quickly discovering she loved the remainder of the house. The place was an odd contrast of delicate beauty and western ruggedness. It made Colleen wonder if the house had once been blended to the taste of Jonas's mother and father.

Minutes later, Jonas entered the room. He'd rolled back the sleeves on his white shirt and removed his tie. The dark hair around his face was damp and a couple of locks fell to their own liking onto his forehead. He was a big man in stature and in presence. He was definitely a man who could be intimidating if he chose to be. But it was the gentle side of Jonas that worried her the most, because that was the part of Jonas she could so easily love.

Love? she thought. How could she even think of the word? Love didn't get you anywhere, especially with men like—

"Go ahead and sit, Colleen, while I bring the dishes in," he told her, interrupting her silent argument.

"I could help," she offered.

He shook his head. "Sit. I won't be but a minute."

Once he had the entire meal on the table, he made another trip to the kitchen. Colleen was surprised when he returned with a bottle of wine and a box of matches.

"For the candles," he told Colleen upon seeing the inquisitive look on her face. He struck a match against the cover, then cupped his palm around the flame while he lit the two slender candles sitting at their end of the long table. Colleen had noticed the candles beforehand but had merely taken them for decoration. She'd never expected him to use them, at least not for a simple supper with her.

"Since you've been ill and are on medication, I'd better not give you any wine. Do you mind if I have some?" he asked as he took a seat at the head of the table, just to her right.

"Please do," she murmured politely, thinking the only other time she'd sat across the table from him was the day he'd bought her truck and they'd shared a cup of coffee. This, however, was far different, she realized. They were alone in an elegant room, the lights were dim and the candleglow flickered on his dark craggy face. Colleen's heart was suddenly a weak rapid flutter under her breast.

"Mmm, this looks good," he said passing her the dish of baked chicken. "I only had time to swallow down a cup of coffee before I had to be in court. I'm surprised the judge didn't fine my growling stomach for contempt."

"Do you have many court appearances?" she asked, curious.

He nodded as he served himself a vegetable. "I take on quite a few criminal cases. Some of my friends think I'm crazy for that, but if I had to read deeds and write wills all the time, I'd never endure being a lawyer."

That didn't surprise her. It was obvious just by looking at him that he was a man of action, a man who had to be doing something he believed in strongly.

"Do you ever have murder cases?"

He grinned, pleased that they could have a pleasant conversation without any arguments or accusations. "A few. Why, are you one of those sleuth, murder mystery readers?"

One side of her mouth lifted faintly. "Sometimes. But that's not the same as real life. I don't think I could bear dealing with the graphic details of such a horrible subject."

Jonas reached for the wine bottle and went to work at pulling out the cork. "The fact is that horrible things happen and sometimes there are innocent people involved. If the defendant is guilty I make certain the DA has proved it beyond a shadow of a doubt. To me and the jury."

"Well, I must admit it all sounds more exciting than raising cattle. Why do you bother with the ranch?"

Surprised, he looked at her. "I live here, Colleen, this is my home. It always has been."

"I know that. But it doesn't necessarily have to be active," she reasoned. "You're obviously making money with your law practice."

A quirk of a smile touched his mouth as he filled his glass with wine, then stuck the cork back into the bottle. "I'm not a Scrooge, Colleen. I don't do it just to see my bank balance rise. I do it because I love the animals, watching the babies grow, watching the land produce, even watching the men enjoy the work they do here. You might not believe it, but I even know how to shovel manure and handle a tractor."

Colleen did believe it. He was the type of man who could do anything he set his mind to. "I know. Rose tells me you're always working here on the ranch."

He sliced into his chicken. "You two have been discussing me?"

Her face was suddenly flooded with color. "Not exactly. She just thinks you work too much and play too little."

His eyes settled on her face as he chewed. "And what do you think?"

She thought absolutely too many things about him. "I think work is necessary to a person's life."

The glint in his gray eyes sparkled back at her. "And what about fun, Colleen? Don't you think that's necessary, too?"

Truthfully Colleen didn't know too much about having fun. She'd never had much time for it, particularly in the past two years while her father had been so terribly ill and needed constant care.

"Maybe someday I'll try it and see," she said with a little smile. "What about you, Jonas? What do you do for fun?"

Shrugging, he sipped his wine. "Count my cows, ride the fenceline, buy a new pair of boots."

Laughter suddenly gurgled up in her throat. She tried to hold it back, but it burst out anyway. "I meant recreation."

He glanced at her as he shoveled his fork full of candied carrots. "That is recreational to me. I'm not a moviegoer, and even though I like fishing and hunting I don't have time for them." He lifted the carrots to his mouth. "I guess my very favorite thing to do is go to a good horse sale."

"Sounds adventurous," she said mockingly.

"It is," he assured her. "Horses are like women, the pretty ones are the first to catch your eye, but they're not necessarily always the best ones. Horses are very hard to judge just by looking at the outside, and so are women. Fickle, frisky, mean, smart, loving, you never know what you're going to get until you've already gotten one home, and by then it's too late. You've already sunk a fortune into her, besides the fact that she's already wormed her way under your skin to the point that even if she kicked you in the head you still couldn't bear to get rid of her."

Colleen reached for her water glass as she mulled over his words. "Not all women or horses are bad," she told him.

Jonas's mouth twisted with a smile as his eyes wandered over her face. For a moment he allowed himself to think of how it would be to have her in his arms, brushing his lips across her smooth skin. Her mouth would be soft, sweet, and full against his. He wondered what it would take to make her lips part with a sigh, what would it take to have her in his bed, willing and waiting for him to make love to her.

Suddenly he frowned down at the glass of burgundy in his hand. "Not all men are bad, either," he admitted. "But I have the suspicion that you wouldn't believe that any more than I believe what you just told me."

Colleen took a bite of her crescent roll. "I don't dislike men, Jonas. I just don't trust them."

Was she going to trust him enough to marry him, Jonas wondered. The question was on the tip of his tongue when the phone in the kitchen began to ring.

"Excuse me, Colleen. That's someone down at the barn or stables. I'd better answer it."

She nodded, grateful for a moment alone so that she could try to put her thoughts in order. But she found that practically impossible to do. She liked being with Jonas, she had to admit that to herself. Even when he was being bossy and opinionated and she was arguing with him, she knew she'd never felt more alive.

Maybe it was because she'd lived alone for so long with no one for company but a flock of sheep and a dog. Perhaps any man would make her feel the same way, she silently reasoned with herself. But Colleen didn't think so. Somehow her heart knew there wasn't any other man on earth like Jonas Dobbs.

At the sound of his footsteps, she looked up to see him standing in the open doorway. "Sorry, Colleen, but I have to run down to the stables. There's a crisis with a foaling mare."

"Of course, Jonas. Would you like for me to wait and finish eating with you?"

He would, but he wasn't going to ask her to. That was something a real husband would ask of his wife, and he couldn't do that. "No, I may be a while. Go ahead without me."

Colleen nodded and was glad he turned quickly and left the room. Otherwise, he might have read the disappointment on her face. He wouldn't have understood it. How could he, when she didn't understand it herself? She did know, however, that he wouldn't like it.

The meal lost some of its flavor without his company. She tried not to think about it and to concentrate on the food. While she ate, her eyes meandered around the room. She tried to imagine eating all her meals in this room, yet it was beyond fathoming for Colleen, and not for the first time today she longed to see Inez.

She wondered what her friend would say about Jonas's unusual proposal. For a long time Inez had wanted Colleen to find a man, get married, have a family. But this was hardly the same thing.

Somehow Colleen didn't think Inez would approve of a marriage for business reasons, any more than she approved of Colleen living alone on a sheep ranch. But Inez didn't understand everything. She would never truly know how hurt and humiliated she'd been when Bradley had turned away from her.

Even though she didn't want it to be that way, the scars still ran deep, and every time she thought of giving herself to another man a cold fear came over her.

When Jonas finally returned to the house he found Colleen in the den watching television. She was sitting on the couch, her knees pulled up under her chin and her hands locked around her ankles. She seemed to be totally involved in the popular detective show, but she looked up as soon as he walked into the room.

"How is the mare?" she asked.

"Fine now. The vet came and turned the colt. After that it was smooth sailing."

Colleen was glad to hear it. She couldn't bear to think of any animal suffering. "Was the colt okay?"

He hitched up his slacks and took a seat beside her. "Beautiful. When you're well enough we'll walk down to the stables and you can see for yourself."

What did that mean? she wondered. That he was just taking it for granted she was going to stay here on the Slash D? "I'd like that," she said, and meant it. "But I'd like even more to get back out to my lambs."

Jonas's gray eyes regarded her keenly. "I'll drive you out for a look in a few days."

"A look?" she echoed with disbelief. "Jonas, this is lambing time. I need to be with the flock."

"Virgil is with them. He knows all about sheep. You couldn't have them in better hands."

"Maybe so, but I'd feel better if I were there, too."

"With Virgil?" he asked, his expression faintly mocking.

Colleen frowned. "With my sheep. Besides," she added, "I have no clothes. I can't continue to wear your mother's, and there's other things I need—"

"I see your point," he interrupted. "Give Rose a list of the 'other things.' She'll get them for you. I'll take care of the clothes."

"Damn it, Jonas, I'm not totally helpless! And I want to go home, make sure everything around the house is okay."

Jonas squared around on the couch so that he was facing Colleen. She didn't have to look down to know there was only an inch or two between his knee and her thigh.

"I've already sent a man out to check on things," he told her.

Instead of reassuring her, his statement angered Colleen even more. "You have to be the boss, don't you? For some crazy reason you want to run my life. My God, what would it be like if we were married? You'd expect me to kowtow to your every word!"

His anger was visible in the flare of his nostrils, the tautening of his jaws, the glitter in his gray eyes. Her first instinct was to shrink away from him, but Colleen wasn't a shrinking violet so she sat there unflinching.

"It's a good thing this won't be a conventional marriage because it's damn sure obvious you could never be a conventional wife."

His accusations hurt, but she wasn't about to let him know, so she hid behind her anger. "And I suppose you think you're perfect husband material?" she asked cuttingly. "Or just perfect for me?"

It was all Jonas could do not to haul her in his arms and shut her up in what he thought would be the most perfect way. "We do have mutual needs," he pointed out with a growl.

Colleen's green eyes traveled all over his angry face. "You think so? Well, right now with your mightier-than-thou act, those needs seem pretty flimsy to me."

If possible his face grew even harder. "Maybe you don't know enough about needs," he gritted. "Maybe I should show you—"

Colleen didn't realize his intentions until he'd already leaned forward and gripped her shoulders. She gasped his name but that was the only word she got out before his lips came down on hers.

The intimate touch shocked her so that for a moment she went stock-still. Yet even as the realization sunk into her mind that he was kissing her, she could not will herself to fight or pull away. His lips were warm, hard and totally tantalizing as they moved over hers.

Jonas heard the tiny moan in her throat, saw the slow descent of her eyelids and knew she was surrendering to him. Just knowing that fueled his desire for her. And it *was* desire he was feeling, he realized. The anger she'd roused in him had vanished as soon as he'd touched her. Now he was discovering that to kiss her, to hold her soft, tender body in his arms did things to him he'd never expected.

Colleen was fast losing her senses. She tried to lever her hands between his chest and herself and push away, but all she could manage to do was grip his shirt front while her lips clung to his, her heart thudding wildly in her chest.

It was Jonas who finally broke away. By then Colleen was limp and starved for air. Drawing in a deep breath, she lifted drowsy eyes up to his face.

Jonas was looking at her as if he didn't know her and was angered to find a stranger in his arms. Colleen supposed it was because he'd never thought of her as a flesh and blood woman before. Now that he had, he was obviously regretting it.

"That wasn't the kind of need I was talking about," she whispered hoarsely, feeling the need to wound him. "Besides, you didn't have to remind me what it's like to kiss a man. I've kissed before. I've even loved before. But I won't be guilty of it again."

Before Jonas could stop her, she jumped from the couch and ran through the house to her room. Once inside it she shut the door and fumbled with the knob, desperately searching for a lock.

Finally she realized there was none and she sank back against the door, frustrated and shaken. For long moments she stood there, her hands covering her face, her mind willing her body to forget him and pull itself back together.

* * *

Jonas fought the urge to go after her. There was nothing he could do, he told himself, nothing he could say to better the situation. No, he'd give her time to calm down, and then he'd—he'd what? Tell her that kissing her had meant nothing to him? Assure her he'd never do it again?

Like hell. Kissing her had meant something to him. To think of never kissing her again was like placing a life sentence on himself. But there wasn't any other choice, he decided grimly. She'd just told him in no uncertain terms she wanted no part of him. And if he expected to live with her and keep an impersonal distance he was going to have to forget all about those moments he'd had her in his arms.

Angry at his own weakness, he choked back a curse and left the couch. At the end of the room, he sat down heavily in his desk chair and reached for a folder jammed with papers. They were filled with information about his upcoming trial. It was going to be a hell of a fight to convince the jury that his client was innocent.

That was good. Because it was going to be an even harder fight to clear his head of Colleen.

For more than an hour Colleen sat in her darkened bedroom, thinking, wondering, agonizing. No matter how she tried, she couldn't understand Jonas's actions, nor could she understand her reaction to him. Her face grew hot every time she thought of the way she'd virtually melted in his arms. She could only hope he hadn't noticed that part. She hoped he'd put her behavior down to that of a sick woman.

Eventually she removed her clothes, donned a nightgown and went to bed. But telling herself to go to sleep was about as futile as banging her head against the wall. No matter what position she lay in, or what she focused her mind on, Jonas's image was always right there staring her in the face.

It was well after midnight when she finally decided to get up. After pulling a thin robe over her gown, she left the bedroom and made her way slowly through the house to the kitchen.

She was heating milk for hot chocolate when Jonas came into the room. The sight of him startled her and her hand involuntarily flew to her throat.

"What are you doing up?" she gasped.

His office clothes were gone. In their place was an old pair of faded jeans and a white undershirt. Her eyes were drawn to his bare arms and shoulders, the black hair curling crisply in the middle of his chest, the outline of his nipples beneath the thin material.

Jonas walked over to where she was tending the pan of milk on the stove. "I've never been to bed," he said, one brow arching at her and the milk. "What are you doing up?"

Her fingers fumbled with the buttons at the throat of her robe, as if to make sure she was completely covered even though he wasn't. "I couldn't sleep. So I got up to make myself a cup of hot chocolate. I hope you don't mind me making myself at home."

Knowing that she hadn't been able to sleep was small compensation for what she'd done to him. For the past five hours he'd been staring at depositions, unable to absorb two whole sentences the entire night. His mind had kept drifting to her, dreaming and wondering about her.

"Of course I don't mind. If we're going to get married—"

Her head jerked up at the last word and Jonas watched her chin jut out in defiance. "I think that's an issue we should settle right now."

"So do I," he said crisply, crossing his arms across his chest.

The action drew Colleen's gaze downward. Once again she was struck by how massively he was built. His arms were corded with muscles that rippled each time he moved. His shoulders and chest were wide and strong-looking, inviting a woman to lean against him. But that particular invitation wasn't for her. She already knew what he did to her, and she couldn't risk it again.

"I want to set things straight right now," he went on. "If you're worried about what happened earlier this evening, you can put your mind to rest. It won't happen again."

Part of Colleen sagged with relief while another wanted to weep with regret. "I'm sure it won't," she told him, forcing her voice to be level and businesslike. "It was obvious from the look on your face that you found me repulsive." She laughed humorlessly.

"But that's not at all surprising. Kissing someone like me has probably been one of your nastier jobs."

Is that what she really thought? Jonas felt anger pouring through him all over again. "I don't consider kissing a job! And after tonight I won't be considering it at all."

The milk was hot. Colleen switched off the burner with unnecessary force. "Good."

"Damn good," he reiterated.

Colleen stirred the dry cocoa mixture into the milk, then poured it into the mug she'd already set out on the cabinet counter. She could feel Jonas's eyes on her as she worked, and she wondered what he was thinking. Maybe he'd decided he didn't want her to be his wife after all. Maybe he'd decided she would be an embarrassment to him. That idea hurt more than she had imagined. Bradley's family had considered her an embarrassment, too, and ultimately she'd lost him. Her self-worth had been crushed back then; she was determined not to let Jonas crush it now.

"So, are you going to marry me?"

His voice was brisk, unemotional, as if he was asking her to ride into town with him rather than asking her to spend the rest of her life as his wife. But then, she reminded herself, emotions didn't enter into any of this.

"Yes, I am."

Colleen couldn't see the pure relief flooding through him. The only outward reaction he made was to let out a breath and lean his hip against the cabinet. "Do you think you'll be ready to stand up before the judge in a couple of days?"

"A couple of days! Are you insane?" she asked, amazed that he was suggesting such a thing.

He frowned and pushed away from the cabinet. Colleen watched him walk across the room to where a coffee maker was set on a small work table. He poured a small amount of the black brew into a fine china cup. "I've never known anyone to continually doubt my sanity like you do," he said tersely.

Colleen carefully cradled the mug between her hands, then took a long sip. "That's because I've never had anyone make such preposterous suggestions to me before."

He moved to the table and pulled out a chair. Colleen watched the denim stretch tightly against his thighs and wondered if his legs were as dark as the rest of him. They were certainly just as muscled.

"Use some sense, Colleen. We don't have much time. How is it going to look if I go into the bank and pay off your notes without us being man and wife?"

"It won't look any worse than you suddenly marrying someone you hardly know," she retorted.

With a distasteful grimace, he set the coffee cup down on the table. "You're wrong. No one is going to know about our past relationship. I've always kept my personal life discreet. For all anyone will know, we've been seeing each other for a long time."

"But Rose—and, my God, your mother. I'm sure she's going to disapprove of this whole set-up."

Jonas regarded her through narrowed eyes. "In her eyes it's not going to be a set-up. It's going to be a normal, loving marriage."

Colleen's mouth popped open. "Oh? And how are we going to manage that? I'm sure your mother is not a dense person. She's going to see right through this."

"Not if you give a good performance."

"Is that what this is, a performance? You told me it was going to be a business deal, nothing more."

He casually reached for his coffee cup. "Between us, it is. When Mother is around we'll have to act like—" he paused, his eyes catching hers "—we care about each other."

Did the man have any idea what he was asking of her?

"I can't do it."

Jonas made an offhand gesture. "Then we'll have to forget the whole thing. My mother wants me to have a loving marriage. I won't hurt her by having her know that you—that it isn't."

Colleen winced sharply. "Don't you mean that I'm just your legal loophole?" She turned her back on him and clutched the mug even tighter. "That's what you lawyers are good at, isn't it? Getting around the obvious?"

"You could call me the same thing," he retorted, then frowned at the look of disapproval in her eyes. "Look, Colleen, we both know that I'm using you. And you're using me."

His bluntness was painful. She turned back around to him. "Yes, but aren't you using me just a little bit more? To deceive your mother—"

"That's better than having her hurt," he broke in. "Besides, she's not here that much, you won't have to play the part of the loving wife but once in a while."

Maybe it would be easier to face his mother with pretense than it would be with the cold truth, she thought. Actually Colleen didn't think she could tell Inez the whole truth of the matter, either. For some illogical reason she wanted her friend to believe she'd finally found a man who loved her.

Colleen pulled out a chair and joined Jonas at the table. "Okay, I'll try my best," she told him. "But I want you to write up one of those premarital agreements saying that my land will always remain mine. As for anything else—well, just because I'll have your name doesn't mean I want anything else that's yours."

This time it was Colleen's bluntness that hurt him. But then he told himself he was reacting crazily. She was saying exactly what he wanted to hear, wasn't she?

"Yes, that's a good idea. I'll write one up in the next few days."

"Before the marriage."

Jonas stared at her. "Colleen, I've got an armed robbery case coming up. It's going to take all my attention for the next few days."

"Then get someone else to write it."

He shook his head at her. "I'll not have every Tom, Dick and Harry knowing about our personal lives.

When I get time I'll write it, we'll both sign it, and I'll keep it under lock and key."

She shot him a wary glance. "And when will you have time?"

"In another week, or two! Hellfire, Colleen, I'm not going to steal your land between now and then!"

"All right, all right," she conceded. "I guess I can trust you until then."

Their eyes met. So this was it, he thought. He was finally going to be married. The fact should have terrified him, but it didn't. Who would have believed that he was actually relieved that Colleen was finally going to belong to him, even if it was in name only?

Chapter Seven

By the next day Colleen's health had greatly improved. She rarely coughed and her strength was returning by leaps and bounds. So much so that she restlessly roamed the house, wishing she could get out and drive to her own ranch.

At least then she might get her mind off the marriage. Earlier today Jonas had called her from his office to tell her he'd made the arrangements for the ceremony to take place the next afternoon in the judge's chambers at the courthouse.

Now all that was left to do was to say, "I do." But each time Colleen thought of it, she began to shake inside.

Impulsively she got up from the couch, switched off the television and picked up the phone from Jonas's desk.

Before she could change her mind she punched out a set of numbers. It rang twice before an unfamiliar female voice answered. "I'd like to speak to Inez please. Tell her it's Colleen."

Colleen could hear the woman yelling out the message above the din of the busy kitchen. Moments later Inez's voice came over the phone.

"Hi, sweetie! This is nice of you to call. Where are you?"

"I'm—are you very busy?"

"Terribly, but don't worry about it. I've always got time to talk to you," Inez said.

Colleen smiled faintly as she smoothed her palm nervously against the edge of the wooden desk. "I just wanted to call and let you know I'm getting married tomorrow."

"What? Janie, turn that damn blender off!" she yelled back into the kitchen. "Did I hear you right? Did you say married?"

Colleen swallowed, hoping she could sound convincing. "Yes."

"My God, who? Who are you marrying? I just saw you a few days ago. If I remember right you still had that man-hater look in your eyes!"

"Inez, I never was a man-hater. Besides, I've met someone and put all that behind me."

"Colleen, who? Who?"

"Jonas Dobbs."

There was a long pause and then in an incredulous voice, she asked, "Jonas Dobbs, the lawyer?"

Colleen almost laughed as she pictured the surprised look on her friend's face. "Yes. That's right."

"Colleen, is this for real? You hardly know the man! Honey, tell me this is some kind of joke."

"I'm very serious, Inez. I'd thought you'd be happy for me. God knows you've preached marriage to me enough for the past five years."

"Happy? Happy! If you were in love I'd be ecstatic. But—"

"What makes you think I'm not?" Colleen asked guardedly.

"Because," she hissed in a low voice that only Colleen could hear, "I know what you went through with Bradley. It would take one hell of a man to make you forget that, and a lot longer than a few days to do it."

Jonas was one hell of a man, Colleen thought, surprising herself. "This is something I've got to do, Inez. Please wish me well."

"Oh, honey," she groaned. "I do. You know I do. I just want this to be right for you."

"It is, believe me. Now I'd better hang up. You will come see me soon, won't you? I'm staying at Jonas's."

"Already?"

Colleen grimaced. Obviously Inez thought that she and Jonas were already having a physical relationship. "It's a long story, Inez. I'll tell you about it later. Come as soon as you can."

"I promise. Love you, honey. Bye, now."

"Goodbye."

"A long story, huh? Who was that?"

Colleen turned around to face Jonas. She moistened her dry lips and pushed away from the desk. "My friend, Inez, from Lake City."

"You told her we were getting married?"

Colleen nodded.

"How did she react?"

"She thinks I must have met a hell of a man to have changed my opinion about men."

"Did you tell her you had?" he asked, an arrogant quirk to his lips.

Her brows lifted to a mocking line. "I led her to believe I had. I thought I'd try lying to her first to see how I could manage it."

Scowling, he took hold of her arm and tugged her out of the room. "Well, you don't have to be so brutally honest with me. You could at least act as if you like me."

His statement surprised her, and for the moment she forgot about where he might be taking her. "I do like you, Jonas, when you're not being bossy," she said, then asked, "Where are we going?"

"To the bedroom. I want to show you something."

He steered her toward the bedroom she'd been occupying since her stay at the ranch. When they entered it, Colleen gasped with surprise at the pile of bags and boxes on the bed. "What in the world?"

"I picked up a few things for you to wear. Next week we'll drive out to your place so you can pack whatever else you'd like to bring back here."

He was being bossy again, but Colleen couldn't find it in her to tell him so. To think that a man had gone out shopping for her was astounding. She went over to the bed and opened a long flat box. In it was a pair of tan slacks with a matching cotton sweater. The next package held a gathered, blue-striped skirt and a white blouse, and the next a sundress with tiny pink roses. There were shoes, scarves, belts, and even a bottle of perfume. It was impossible for her to refrain from opening the stopper and dabbing the sultry scent on her throat and behind her ears.

Finally she looked over her shoulder to see Jonas was watching her intently. She felt her heart give a lurch, then speed ahead. "Jonas—this was totally unnecessary. I have clothes at home."

He shrugged. "You're going to be married. And all brides are supposed to have a trousseau."

Her eyes dropped from his as a pain ran through her. "I'm not a traditional bride," she reminded them both. Reaching down, she lightly fingered a soft blouse done in pink georgette. She'd never owned anything like it, and even if she had there wouldn't have been any place or time for her to wear it. "But I guess you knew my clothes wouldn't be appropriate for the Slash D."

His mouth tightened to a thin line. "Damn it, Colleen, don't act pathetic with me! I don't care what you wear around here just as long as you're not naked! I bought the clothes because I wanted to do something nice for you. But I guess you're always going to question my motives."

Jonas's anger touched her in a strange way. Perhaps she was behaving defensively, she thought. But didn't he understand this was all happening too quickly for her? She wasn't used to his sort of lifestyle. Even more, she wasn't used to him.

With a frustrated sigh, she glanced up at him. "I'm—not used to anyone buying me things," she tried to explain. "Anyway, thank you, Jonas. I do like everything."

He slanted her a dry look as though he wasn't quite sure of her sincerity, then moved over to a bureau where another box was lying. Colleen hadn't noticed it before, and she looked at it curiously as Jonas lifted the lid.

"You're probably going to be mad about this, too," he told her, "but I bought it, anyway. I figured you couldn't stay angry at me forever."

Forever. Were they really going to be together forever? Colleen didn't have time to ponder the question. She suddenly gasped as Jonas held up a dress. It was an exquisite sheath done in ivory taffeta overlaid with ivory lace.

"Of course," he went on before she could respond, "if you'd like to exchange it for something else, Rose will run you into town. I do realize that it's your wedding, too, and you might like to make your own choices."

Colleen was suddenly overwhelmed. She hadn't expected him to regard the legal ceremony as a wedding. "It's beautiful," she said quietly. "But isn't it a bit—" she wanted to say romantic, but couldn't bring herself to "—a bit too much?" she said. "I mean, since this is just a legal thing and not a traditional marriage."

Jonas wished he'd never used that word. He was getting damn tired of hearing it. "Colleen, let's get this straightened out right now. Just because this is a different type of marriage, it doesn't mean we can't be nice to each other, or do things for each other."

The kindness on his face made it impossible for Colleen to resist him. Smiling broadly, she reached out and quickly plucked the dress from his hands then held it up against her.

"It's gorgeous, Jonas. Truly gorgeous."

Jonas smiled to himself, amazed at how good it felt to please her. "Go try it on," he urged.

"Oh no! It would be unlucky for you to see me in it," she said, unaware that she was blushing and behaving like a true bride. "You'll have to wait until tomorrow."

The next day came and went like a dream for Colleen. They were married before the judge, whom Jonas seemed to know quite well. The DA, another friend of Jonas, was a witness, along with Rose, who'd practically begged Jonas to be one.

The ceremony was short and to the point. After the judge had pronounced them man and wife, Jonas had given her a lingering kiss that had taken her by surprise. But then she'd told herself he'd done it to make things look real in front of his friends. Just like the nosegay of pink-and-white roses he'd given her to carry.

Afterward, they'd driven back to the ranch where Jonas called up the hands from the stables and broke out several bottles of champagne while Rose passed around hors d'oeuvres. Much to Colleen's surprise he seemed to be in a festive mood, and the small gathering had told her much about Jonas's character. He considered those who worked for him as his friends and obviously didn't put himself above them.

Colleen supposed it was a wedding day like most others, except there had been no love behind the vows they'd spoken to each other, only legality. But throughout the day she'd smiled and pretended that Jonas was in love with her and she with him. It had been easy to do when he'd had his arm around her shoulders, or held her hand in his.

But the magic of the wedding day faded away that night when he'd gone to his bedroom and she to hers. For some inexplicable reason she'd cried long and hard in the dark loneliness of her room.

Two days later Inez came to visit. Colleen was so glad to see her friend that she gave her a long, tearful hug.

Finally, Inez put Colleen away from her and critically examined every inch of her. "You look thin and pale," she said disapprovingly.

Colleen waved away her words and began leading her toward the kitchen. "That's because I've been ill with bronchitis. But I'm almost over that now."

"Ill! You didn't say anything about that on the telephone."

"It was too long a story. Jonas came out to the camp and found me. I was out of my head with fever."

"Good Lord! See what I told you about being out there alone? At least I won't have to worry about that anymore."

Rose was busy in the kitchen, mixing up yeast dough for dinner rolls. Colleen introduced the two women. They took an instant liking to each other, just as Colleen suspected they would. Once the housekeeper discovered Inez ran a restaurant, the two of them began to exchange cooking stories and recipes.

Colleen was content to sit quietly listening while she sipped a tall glass of iced tea. It was enough for her to know that these two people cared about her and wanted to be in her company.

Eventually Rose went down to the basement to finish the laundry. Inez helped herself to more tea, then plopped down in the chair next to Colleen's. "All right, honey, I want to hear everything."

Colleen tossed her friend an innocent look. "About what?"

"You know about what! Jonas Dobbs! This marriage!" Her eyes darted around the room. "I never expected to see you living in a place like this."

"I never expected to live in a place like this," Colleen said truthfully.

"What is he like, this Jonas of yours?"

What would Inez think if she knew that Jonas belonged to Colleen in name only? Colleen traced an imaginary figure on the tabletop. "He's intelligent. Handsome. Nice when he wants to be."

"Colleen! Those aren't the things a bride says about her new husband! I thought I was going to hear a bunch of gush. Like he's wonderful, he's so romantic, he makes me crazy in bed."

Colleen blushed, partly because she was hiding the truth, and partly because she wished she *could* say those things.

"Well, I said all that," Colleen said defensively. "It just wasn't in a gushy way."

Inez rolled her eyes. "Do you love him?"

Of course she didn't love Jonas. She couldn't. But why was a voice urging her to say, yes, yes! The voice scared her, and she desperately tried to ignore it. "Inez, why do you have to be so blunt? Anyway, you've badgered me for years about getting married. You should be pleased."

Inez gave her a pointed look. "I am as long as you are."

Colleen let out a sigh of relief, then forced a broad smile on her face. "Of course I am. I have a beautiful home and a successful husband. I'm planning on it lasting forever."

But what was it that was going to last forever, Colleen asked herself once Inez had left. There was nothing to her marriage. It was just an empty shell of a thing without love or children to fill it.

That evening Jonas found Colleen in her bedroom brushing her hair. She was wearing the pink sundress he'd bought her. It showed off her delicate collarbone and the slenderness of her arms and shoulders. He'd never thought he cared for short hair on a woman, but each time he looked at Colleen he found it particularly appealing. He liked the way it exposed the tender nape of her neck and the long lines of her throat. He liked the way the fluff of red-gold bangs fell across her forehead and made her green eyes appear even greener.

Trying to push the intimate thoughts away, he strolled into the room. Stopping behind her, his eyes met hers in the dressing mirror. "Ready for supper?" he asked.

He never knocked, and Colleen looked at him, wondering what he would think if he came in and found her undressed. Probably nothing, she thought, ruefully.

"Hello," she said, then rose from the dressing bench. "Yes. I'm ready whenever you are."

The sultry scent of the perfume he'd given her swirled around her as she moved past him. Jonas wondered if it had been masochistic to buy it.

"I went by the bank today and paid your loans," he said, following her out the door.

Surprised, Colleen glanced over her shoulder at him. "Didn't I need to be there, too?"

"Not really. Since I'm your husband, they were more than happy for me to write them a check. I have copies of the notes marked paid in my briefcase. You might want to hold them for safekeeping."

"Yes, thank you. I will." The knowledge that her land was debt-free should have filled her with happiness, but it didn't. She kept thinking of the price it had cost her to keep it. And of how it was going to be to live out the rest of her life with a man that didn't love her.

Once they were seated and eating, Colleen brought up the subject of the land again. "Jonas, what are we going to do now?"

He glanced up at her from beneath his thick lashes. He had beautiful gray eyes, she decided. And because his skin was so dark their color was virtually startling. In spite of herself, she found her own eyes drawn to them again and again.

"What do you mean?" he asked.

"The land. My land. Your land. We have two pieces now. How are they going to fit together?"

Jonas wondered if she was talking about him and her, and not the land. Could they somehow fit together as lovers, as true man and wife? The idea left him shaken.

Colleen mistook the nagging frown on his forehead as anger. She stiffened in her seat as she waited for him to answer.

"I don't know," he finally said. "I haven't really thought about it. We could tear down the boundary fence between us, but if you want to keep your sheep, we'd have to do something different. You know as well as I that sheep and cattle don't mix."

"I do want to keep my sheep," she said crisply. He may have paid her way out, but she wasn't going to give up everything because of it.

Sensing her belligerence, Jonas felt himself go cold all over. She was just like Lana, he thought sickly. Each time he told himself she couldn't be, she stuck her chin in the air and reminded him that her life was her own and that she was going to keep it separate from him. It must be some kind of curse, he decided, that drew him to the wrong kind of woman.

"Naturally, I won't expect you to invest in the welfare of my sheep," he heard her saying. "I'll keep a separate set of books on them, so it won't cause you any problems."

She was already causing problems, he told himself. She had the power to anger and hurt him, and they'd only been married a few days. If he didn't get a handle on his feelings what would it be like after a few weeks, a few months?

"I suppose you'd also like for me to put all this in the premarital agreement?" he asked tersely.

Colleen gave him one short nod. "That way there won't be any misunderstanding."

Jonas took pleasure in stabbing the chicken breast on his plate. "By all means, Colleen, let's get everything down in black and white. We wouldn't want to get too personal or actually trust one another about any of this."

Colleen gripped her fork and paid close attention to the food on her plate. Maybe she did sound cold and unfeeling, but she had to look out for herself. Jonas didn't care about her, much less her lambs. If she couldn't hold on to them and her land, this whole farce of a marriage would be pointless.

For the next week Jonas worked continually on the armed robbery case. But he managed to take time out to show Colleen around the barns and stables, and one evening he'd taken her out in an open-top Jeep to show her a part of the ranch. Colleen had enjoyed the outing more than she'd liked to admit. So much so that when he'd invited her to come to the courthouse today to hear his closing argument, she'd declined.

Colleen knew if she was going to be able to keep her heart distanced from him, she would have to stay away from him as much as possible. That was the only way it could be.

Just after lunch Colleen was in her room pulling on a lavender shirt and a pair of jeans when she heard voices coming from the front of the house.

Thinking it might be Inez, she quickly ran a brush through her hair and started toward the entrance. As she hurried down the hallway, she met Rose and another woman coming toward her.

"Oh, there you are, Colleen," Rose said excitedly. "Look who's finally come home! This is Jonas's mother, Juanita."

From the earlier description Rose had given her, she'd guessed as much. Juanita was a beautiful woman.

"How do you do, Mrs. Dobbs?" Colleen said politely.

Juanita's dark eyes ran warmly over Colleen's slender figure. "Oh, my dear, you're so lovely!"

Before Colleen guessed the woman's intentions she felt herself being pulled into a tight embrace. "Jonas told me over the phone you were pretty!" she exclaimed. "But I didn't realize he meant this pretty!"

Dazed, Colleen could only smile at the woman. "Jonas exaggerated," she said finally. "Did you have a safe trip home?"

Juanita nodded. "Yes, fine. Rose, would you bring us a pot of coffee in the den? And anything sweet if you have it. I've dieted for the past five days. I don't think I can go another second without eating something with sugar in it."

"Coming right up," Rose said with a laugh as she turned off in the direction of the kitchen.

"Well, now, first of all," Juanita said, linking her arm through her new daughter-in-law's, "I'm just furious with my son for not letting me know about the wedding. And to think he's been keeping your romance a secret. Well! But, oh, it's so wonderful to know he finally has someone to love."

Juanita sighed with happiness, and Colleen wanted to sink into the floor. "Yes, I know what you mean."

The two of them entered the den and both took a seat on the long chesterfield. Colleen felt as if she were staring at the woman, but Juanita was so strikingly attractive. She was dressed in a peach-colored shift cinched in at the waist with a turquoise and silver belt. A beautifully crafted turquoise and silver squash blossom necklace hung from her neck and adorned the plain bodice. Her sleek black hair was caught back from her face and coiled into a cool French twist.

Colleen felt dowdy in comparison, and wished she'd never changed into her jeans. "I tried to get Jonas to wait until you got home to have the wedding, but he wanted to surprise you."

Juanita laughed easily. "That's just a nice way of saying he didn't want me here prying my nose in and making it into a big affair." She smiled at Colleen. "It doesn't matter anyway. I'm very happy about the two of you."

"Thank you. I hope you'll not be disappointed in me."

Juanita looked surprised. "My dear, as long as you keep my son happy, that's all that matters."

Rose entered with a tray of coffee and sliced chocolate cake. As she handed out the plates and cups to the two women, Juanita went on, "He was hurt so badly in the past that his father and I were terribly afraid he would never fall in love again. But I kept hoping that someday he'd meet a woman who could make him forget all that."

Rose cocked a pointed look at Colleen that said even though the housekeeper knew Colleen and Jonas slept in separate beds, she didn't want Juanita to know it.

"Yes, Jonas told me about Lana." She didn't know what else to say.

Juanita frowned as she took a sip of her coffee. "She was a cold-blooded woman. She led Jonas to believe she wanted marriage, children, a life together. But then when the time came for the real commitment she turned her back on him. But enough about that horrible time—what about you, Colleen? Jonas tells me you raise sheep."

Relieved that the subject had been changed so easily, Colleen answered enthusiastically. "Yes, my ranch is just south of here. Well, actually it connects to Jonas's back boundary fence." Ranching was an impersonal subject she could talk comfortably about, without being reminded of Jonas and how he'd been hurt by love. How he'd told her he'd never love again.

"My goodness, that goes all the way to the mountains," Juanita observed.

Colleen nodded. "My father died this past year. Since then I'd been living out there alone."

"Is there anything else you want, Juanita?" Rose asked.

"No thank you, Rose, this is lovely. But I should apologize to Colleen. I've come in here and taken over like I'm still the mistress of the place. Please forgive me, Colleen, it's from habit over all these past years."

Blushing, Colleen shook her head. She didn't feel as if she were the mistress of the Slash D any more than Rose was. "There's no need to explain. This has been your home far longer than mine. I hope you'll still continue to think of it that way."

"You're so sweet. No wonder Jonas immediately fell in love with you."

Obviously Jonas must have really spread it on for his mother's benefit, she thought. "Is that what he said?"

Juanita's smile was glowing with happiness. "I think it was something like love at first sight. He told me he'd met you long ago when you were only a teenager, but that you saw each other again for the first time out at your sheep camp."

Why couldn't he have lied about that, too? she wondered. "He shouldn't have told you that. It would have sounded much better if he'd said the theater or a party."

"Nonsense," Juanita said with a laugh. "I think it's wonderful that you're not one of those social flowers. Besides, I can't imagine Jonas being happy with a woman like that at all. Jonas is a man of substance, and I always felt like he'd want a woman like that, too."

Colleen leaned back against the couch and sliced into her cake. She was beginning to like Juanita Dobbs.

Juanita sipped her coffee, then placed the cup and saucer onto the low table in front of them. Looking at Colleen she smiled gently. "You can't imagine how excited I am about having grandchildren. Of course, I know I'm jumping the gun. You've only been married for a few days, but when the time comes I know you and Jonas will make wonderful parents."

Colleen's eyes fluttered down as a sick feeling struck her. What would it do to this lovely woman if she discovered what her son's marriage was really all about? It would devastate her to know there would never be grandchildren.

The two women had been chatting for an hour or so when Jonas entered the room, surprising them both.

"Jonas, isn't the trial going on?" Colleen asked.

He walked to the end of the room and tossed down his briefcase. "The jury only deliberated twenty minutes before they came back with a not guilty verdict."

Colleen quickly rose to her feet and went to him. "That's wonderful, darling," she told him, raising up on tiptoe to kiss his cheek.

The curious look in his eyes was discernible only to Colleen, yet it was enough to tell her he was surprised at her warm greeting.

With a devilish little smile he put his arms around her waist and drew her close against him. Colleen felt heat rush to her face as he bent his head and kissed her thoroughly.

Juanita beamed at the two of them. "This is wonderful news, Jonas. I've been keeping up with the trial in the papers. I was beginning to wonder if you'd be able to pull it off."

Jonas chuckled, obviously pleased with himself. "The papers nailed my client because he'd served a short prison term in the past. But I proved to them that people do have a change of heart."

"Most people think once a criminal, always a criminal," Colleen said, slipping out of Jonas's embrace and returning to her seat on the couch.

Juanita patted the space between Colleen and herself. "Come here and have some coffee with us," she invited her son. "I'd like to hear how you managed to convince the jury."

He went over to the couch, sat down close to Colleen and rested his hand on her knee. Her body reacted strongly to the casual touch and she struggled to keep it from showing on her face.

"I merely pointed out that you can't convict someone simply on their past, that there has to be hard-core evidence, which the DA failed to come up with."

Colleen looked up at him. His face was only inches away and she felt her breath stop in her throat. "Do you really think a person is capable of that kind of change?" she asked.

His eyes moved from hers, down her straight nose to rest on her full lips. "I proved it today, didn't I?"

His gaze was a caress in itself, sending a shiver down her spine. "No, you only proved you're a good lawyer."

Juanita laughed. "Oh, I can already see that Colleen will keep you on your toes, Jonas."

He smiled wryly and helped himself to Colleen's coffee. Somehow it seemed such an intimate thing to see his lips on the same spot hers had been, and suddenly she was thinking of his kiss.

"And I can already see that I'm going to be ganged up on," he said with fondness, then glanced over at his mother. "You are going to stay for supper, aren't you, Mother?"

Colleen held her breath. She liked Jonas's mother, but she didn't know about having Jonas this close to her for an entire evening.

"I shouldn't really, Jonas. Newlyweds don't need a third party around, especially a relative."

Jonas smiled sexily into Colleen's eyes. "We can control ourselves for that long, can't we, Honey?"

Colleen's face blushed beet red and she promised herself she'd murder him later. "I think I can manage, if you can, Darling."

Juanita chuckled. "Well, if you're both sure. I would love to visit a little longer."

Colleen smiled warmly at Juanita, while silently thinking she'd be able to go into acting after this evening was over.

Chapter Eight

As it turned out, Juanita left right after supper. She'd hardly gotten out of the house when Jonas was called down to the barn to straighten out a problem with a piece of haying equipment.

Feeling strangely restless, Colleen went out to the deck and sank down onto a chaise lounge. The night was still warm and the sky strung with countless stars. She leaned her head back and studied them while her thoughts traveled to the mountains.

She figured the sheep were bedded down by now and the mountains would be quiet. Since Jonas didn't possess a sheepdog, Dangit had gone back out to the camp with Virgil. Colleen missed the dog terribly. He'd been her closest companion for a long time. It didn't seem the same without the dog by her side.

Especially since he'd shown her much more affection than Jonas did, she thought bemusedly.

The soft swish of the glass patio door warned her that she was no longer alone. Glancing around, she saw Jonas walking across the planked deck toward her.

"You shouldn't be breathing the night air," he said, taking a seat on the end of her lounger.

It amazed Colleen how overprotective he was at times. "Nonsense. I've been over the bronchitis for days now."

He reached over and took her hand between both of his. "I want to thank you," he said, "for being so wonderful with Mother. She left here tonight adoring you."

Her heart thudded as she studied his profile in the near darkness. "It was easy to be nice to your mother. I like her very much." She looked away from him and let out a weary sigh. "I guess that's why it makes me so ashamed to deceive her."

Had it really been all deception? Jonas asked himself. Over the past few hours it had almost felt as if they were truly man and wife, proud of each other, committed and completely in love. It had left him with a warm, contented feeling. It shocked him to realize he didn't want to give that up just because his mother was not around.

Slowly his fingers brushed across the back of her hand. The skin was a bit softer now, her nails painted a soft peach color. In that way it was different than the hands he'd first noticed out at the sheep camp. Yet they were still the same small, vulnerable hands he'd wanted to reach out and hold.

"Don't think of it as deceiving, Colleen. It would hurt her more to know the truth."

Colleen blinked as unexpected tears stung her eyes. It was more than just deceiving his mother. She might as well admit it to herself. She wanted this marriage to Jonas to be real. When he touched her, she wanted it to be because he wanted to. She wanted to know that the tender look in his eyes was coming from his heart.

"And what do you think it's going to do to her when we don't give her a grandchild?"

Her question surprised him. "Where did that come from? I didn't hear her mention us having children."

Colleen swallowed, trying to control her feelings. "She talked to me about it earlier. She seems to think we'd be wonderful parents," she said bitterly. Her mouth twisted as she added, "I guess after a certain length of time passes we can tell her one of is sterile."

His hold tightened on her hand. "I—I'm sorry about that, Colleen. I know how much you're against having children." He paused, and he began to absently twist the gold wedding band back and forth on her finger. "Frankly, I can't imagine a woman who loves little lambs not wanting or loving a child of her own."

Aghast, she jerked her hand from his grasp. "Is that what you think? That I wouldn't want or love a child?"

Her voice quivered with hurt and outrage. Jonas didn't know what to think, and he searched her face for an answer. "I didn't mean it that way, Colleen. Lots of women just aren't the maternal type, or they have a career to consider—" He broke off impatiently, then shook his head. "I don't understand you, Colleen. You told me you didn't want children."

Tears were in her eyes before she could stop them. As Jonas watched them spill onto her cheeks he felt a part of his heart rip.

"Not because I wouldn't love one," she said hoarsely, then, with a tiny sob, she pressed her fists against her eyes. "I don't want to talk about this anymore, Jonas."

Scooting up beside her, Jonas curled his hands around her shoulders. "But I do," he said, gently. "I want to know why you have this thing about men, why you never want to have a child."

Colleen felt the terrible coldness come over her as it always did when she thought about her past. It helped harden what little resistance she had against him. "It's none of your business," she said flatly.

Frustrated, he gave her shoulders a slight shake. "It is my business. I'm your husband!"

She looked at him mockingly. "Since when?"

"Since right now!" he growled, pushing her down against the lounge and pinning her with his broad chest. "So you either tell me about it, or get ready to spend the night right here."

Her nostrils flared with anger as she struggled and pushed at his broad chest, but after a moment she realized it was as futile to fight him physically as it was to fight the feelings in her heart. Sagging with defeat she looked up at his dark face hovering over hers.

"You asked for this, so I'll tell you," she said wearily. "I loved a man once. We met in college. His name was Bradley Gordon."

Jonas hadn't known she'd ever been to college, much less fallen in love. It put an altogether different light on things. "What happened?" he prompted.

Her eyes unconsciously pulled away from his. "We dated for nearly a year, and we fell in love. Bradley asked me to marry him and we were on the verge of becoming engaged." She stopped and swallowed as the pain and humiliation of that time swelled up inside her. "Then Bradley took me home to meet his parents. They took one look at me and decided that their son deserved better than a sheep herder's daughter."

It infuriated Jonas to think that anyone had ever looked down at Colleen. "So, didn't Bradley have a mouth? He should have defended you. If he loved you—"

Her mouth a grim line, she shook her head. "The Gordons swore that if Bradley didn't stop seeing me they'd cut off all his funds and sever his inheritance." She gave a bitter snort. "In the meantime, I discovered Roger was a friend of the Gordon's, and I have a pretty good suspicion he encouraged them to get me out of Bradley's life."

Jonas frowned with confusion. "Roger? But why would he do something like that?"

She let out a long breath. "You have to understand that there's always been bad feelings between our two families. Even though Roger's mother and my father were brother and sister, they were never close. She always regarded my father as an outcast and an embarrassment to the family. When Grandfather died and willed all his land to Dad instead of Roger's mother, it cut the rift even deeper."

No wonder Roger was so hot to get his hands on Colleen's land, Jonas thought, then asked, "I take it Bradley suddenly decided he wasn't in love after all?"

Colleen nodded silently.

A few seconds passed as Jonas digested the whole thing. "Well, you were better off without someone as shallow as Bradley Gordon. Surely you could see that."

"A nineteen-year-old girl can't see too plainly when her heart is breaking. Especially when she's pregnant and the man has turned away from her," Colleen told him.

"Pregnant! My God, Colleen!"

Her voice quivering, she said, "I lost the baby in the third month. Dad said it was a blessing, but I'd never felt so empty in my life. After that I forgot about college and decided that staying on the ranch and raising sheep was the best life for me after all."

"So you see," she finished, "it's all rather ironic. Bradley left me to keep his inheritance, and you married me to hold on to yours. I guess I didn't learn much after all."

Jonas couldn't bear for her to think that. He couldn't bear for them to keep living with this indifference.

"Don't say that. It's not true!"

"It's like you said, Jonas. We're using each other."

"Damn it, Colleen, if all I wanted was to keep my land I could have married anyone!"

Colleen went very still. "What are you trying to say?"

He couldn't go back now. Moreover he didn't want to. He wanted their life to be together. Really together. "It wasn't the idea of saving my land that kept drawing me to you, Colleen."

"I don't believe that," she whispered.

"Then believe this," he muttered, lowering his head down to hers.

Colleen's gasp was stifled by his mouth on hers. But her surprise was quickly replaced with desire. For so long she'd tried to fight her feelings for him, but his warm mouth plundering hers released a dam inside her. She wanted this. She wanted him. It was impossible to hide it any longer.

Groaning, he shifted, drawing her closer so that her small breasts were pressed against him. Just the feel of her body against him made him crazy for her, and he realized that a part of him had wanted this from the first time he'd seen her. He'd just refused to acknowledge it.

His mouth tore away from hers then slid against her throat, tasting the sweetness of her skin.

"Jonas..." she whispered brokenly, "don't hurt me."

Wanting desperately to reassure her, he buried his hands in her hair and cradled her head. "I could never hurt you, Colleen. I want to love you . . . like this . . . forever," he said, softly nipping her cheeks, her chin and finally her lips.

How could she doubt the passion in his touch, the fervor in his voice? She couldn't, because she wanted him too much, needed his love more than anything she'd ever needed in her life.

"I want to believe that, Jonas."

Cupping the sides of her face between his palms, he held her head motionless as his mouth savored every curve of her lips.

Colleen sighed mindlessly when his mouth finally pulled away from hers and nuzzled the tender skin behind her ear.

"You're my wife, Colleen. I want it to be in every way. You can trust me."

His fingers began to work at the buttons on her blouse. Colleen shivered as the pieces of cloth fell away and cool air brushed across her heated skin. She held her breath in anticipation as his hands touched her midriff ever so softly, then slowly slid upward until his palms were cupping both breasts.

Colleen arched upward toward his touch, the tiny moan in her throat expressing the pleasure surging through her.

She'd never expected or dreamed that he'd ever be touching her like this or saying words of love to her. Now that he was, she felt transported to a wonderful new dimension.

"Colleen, you're so soft, so precious." His lips brushed across the tops of her breasts, then with agonizing slowness his tongue circled first one nipple then the other, bringing a groan of sweet agony from Colleen's lips. "I want to make love to you," he whispered hoarsely. "I want to make you my wife."

Colleen couldn't deny him. To do so would be like denying her own heart. "Yes, Jonas," she whispered.

Quickly, without speaking, he pulled her to her feet and guided her into the house. In the dimly lit hallway he stopped long enough to draw her back in into his arms and plunder her mouth again.

The urgency of his embrace left her legs weak and trembling. Colleen clung to him, gasping his name in the darkness.

Jonas swung her up into his arms and started down the hallway to the bedroom. Colleen hugged his neck tightly, thinking of all the past nights they'd lain across the hallway from each other, so near and yet so far away. It wouldn't be like that tonight. She hoped it would never be like that again.

In the bedroom he stood her on her feet beside the bed. The room was dark, Colleen worked open the buttons on his shirt by touch, and pushed the shirt from Jonas's shoulders. He was a magnificent mass of muscle and bone and she reveled in the feel of him beneath her exploring fingers.

In turn, Jonas slowly removed her blouse, then her jeans, exposing her tall slender body in its dainty lace underwear. "God, you're beautiful, Colleen," he murmured huskily, his hands spanning her small waist.

She moved against him, lifting her arms up to circle his neck. It was amazing how much she wanted him, how much of herself she wanted to give him.

He lifted her onto the wide bed, then stepped back to remove his jeans and boots. Once they were tossed aside, Colleen held her arms out to him.

It was the most trusting, inviting thing Jonas could imagine her doing, and his heart sang out a rapid beat as he went to her.

The sun was already high in the sky when Colleen awoke the next morning. She was on her side, one cheek buried in the pillow. Jonas's warm body was pressed up against her back, his arm slung possessively over her hips.

For a long time she lay there with her eyes closed, letting the memories of the past night wash through her like a welcome rain. Jonas had made love to her so tenderly and completely that she was certain everything about her had changed. She couldn't be the same woman she'd been yesterday. She felt too gloriously happy to be that same Colleen.

Twisting her head on the pillow she looked into Jonas's face and discovered that he was also awake. "Good morning," she said, smiling sleepily at him.

"Good morning, my darling," he told her, drawing her around and into his arms. "Do you know what it's like finding you here beside me this morning?"

She snuggled against his chest, a smile on her face as she buried it in his neck. "Shocking."

His chest shook with a chuckle. "Besides that," he said.

"No. Tell me."

Beneath his hand, her skin was like soft satin as he stroked from her shoulder to hip and back again. Last night he'd discovered his wife was the most passionate, giving woman he'd ever known. Just looking at her now stirred his desire. "Wonderful. I don't want to move, ever."

"Ever? Do you suppose Rose would come feed us if we didn't?"

His voice was lazy and teasing as he said, "I'd fire her if she didn't."

"You're terrible," she scolded softly.

He laughed and nuzzled his nose against the side of her neck. The movement brought her arms up and around his neck.

"Terribly in love," he told her, "with a beautiful strawberry-blonde."

Suddenly a tiny pang of fear rushed through her and she closed her eyes and pressed her cheek against his neck. It scared her to be this happy. She kept thinking of Bradley and how he'd ended up abusing her love. She couldn't bear to think that Jonas might ultimately do that, too.

"Jonas, I love you," she whispered fervently.

"I know. You told me last night," he said in a complacent voice.

"I did?"

His hands moved across her back, pressing her even closer against him. "In a thousand ways. But come here and tell me again, anyway."

She propped herself upon his chest and looked deeply into his eyes. "I love you, Jonas. And all those things I said about the premarital agreement—well, I don't want it. I don't want anything to be between us now. I mean, of course I don't expect what's yours to become mine, but I trust you with—"

The rough features of his face suddenly softened. "Colleen. Colleen, darling," he quickly cut in, "as far as I'm concerned, last night you became my wife completely. And that's the way it will always be. What do you say we combine our ranches in some way?"

She nodded happily. "Surely lambs and calves can mix if we work hard enough."

Smiling he pulled her head down to his. "I love you, my little lamb. Come here and let me show you."

He captured her mouth in a devouring kiss and desire fresh and new poured through Colleen.

With a groan, Jonas quickly turned her onto her back while his hands cupped her breasts. Colleen shifted restlessly, knowing she'd never get enough of this man, her husband. Just knowing that he belonged to her made her drunk with desire.

"I think," he said, after giving her another soul-stirring kiss, "that I'll call Opal and tell her to cancel all my appointments for today."

Colleen smiled as he reached for the phone beside the bed. "Are you sure one day will be enough?" she asked provocatively.

His eyes squinted down at her and his mouth curved into a sexy twist. "You're right. I'd better make it two."

A week later, Colleen drove into Gunnison to meet Jonas for lunch. Her face glowed with happiness as she walked down the sidewalk, window-shopping while waiting for her husband.

The past week had been wonderful. With each passing day she and Jonas had grown closer together. She was head over heels in love with him, and she truly believed that he loved her, too. He was already talking about scheduling out two weeks at his law office so they could take a real honeymoon on the Texas coast. And yesterday he'd brought home a diamond engagement ring. To go with her gold wedding band, he'd told her.

Colleen still hadn't quite gotten over it, and she glanced down every so often at the shiny stone on her finger. The sight of it made her mouth curve into a smile, for it was as new and brilliant as her love for Jonas.

"Well, fancy meeting you here."

At the sound of the male voice, Colleen turned away from the department store window. Her cousin, Roger Boyd, was standing on the sidewalk a few steps away.

She couldn't have been more shocked to see him in Gunnison. "Roger?"

His smile was faintly condescending and Colleen studied him coolly beneath the brim of her straw sunhat.

"So you remember your cousin after all," he said dryly.

He was wearing a light-colored summer suit and his blond hair was brushed and sprayed in a perfect side part. In Colleen's opinion he was overdone, especially for a relaxed western town like Gunnison. But then, Roger had always wanted to stand out from the pack.

"I couldn't possibly forget you, Roger. There could only be one like you."

His smile turned cat-like. "I'll take that as a compliment, Colleen," he said, his eyes running up and down the length of her. She was dressed in a straight white skirt and white pumps. A cool blue blouse of whisper-soft chiffon complemented her strawberry-blond hair.

"You're looking well, Colleen. Actually, I'm surprised to find you here in town. I thought you'd be out on the mountain baby-sitting your lambs."

She gave him a sober look. "They're being looked after."

He grinned, as though her coolness didn't affect him in the least. "This is really rather fortunate that I spotted you," he said. "It saves me the trouble of driving out to your place."

Colleen suddenly understood why he was here, and she quickly had to remind herself that he couldn't hurt her now. "To talk about my land, no doubt," she said with a tight grimace.

He hooked his thumbs over his belt and continued to study her in what Colleen considered a patronizing way. "Jonas said you didn't want to sell. But, frankly, I can't believe that. I know you need money, Colleen. I know that lazy father of yours—"

"Don't speak of my father," she interrupted furiously. "You never bothered yourself to know the man."

"Grandfather should have left that land to my mother, not Uncle Wilton. He was content to sit back and watch the world go by. At least Mother would have put it to good use."

Yeah, like sold it and squandered the money, Colleen thought angrily. "I'll just bet," she gritted out.

Roger held up both hands in a pleading gesture. "All right, let's forget about the past and talk about now. We both know your father left you in sad shape. I'm here to help you out."

It was nearing noon and the sun was beating down on them. But Colleen was cold with fury. "You wouldn't help your own mother unless you thought you could make a profit."

He chuckled and made a clucking sound with his tongue. "And since when did you become Miss High-and-Mighty?"

Colleen let out a long breath and pointedly glanced down at her watch. "I'm sorry to end this lovely reunion, Roger, but I'm meeting my husband for lunch."

She glanced back up at him and almost wanted to laugh. He looked as though he'd been shot between the eyes.

"Husband? You're kidding, aren't you? I've never heard of you looking at a man since—"

"Bradley?" she finished harshly. "You would know about that, wouldn't you?"

He waved away her words. "That was a long time ago. Who is this guy, anyone I know?"

He'd finally asked a question she could smile about. "Of course, you do. It's Jonas."

Roger's mouth gaped open like a dying fish. "Jonas?"

Colleen nodded, then turned to leave. "Goodbye, Roger. Have a safe trip back to Kansas," she told him over her shoulder.

"Like hell," he suddenly spat. "That bast—he cheated me!"

The strange accusation made Colleen halt her steps and turn around. "Who cheated you, Roger?" she demanded.

If he was accusing Jonas of something she was going to let him have it with both barrels.

"Jonas Dobbs, my so-called friend!"

Colleen hitched the strap of her purse farther up her shoulder while she glared at her cousin. "Jonas wouldn't cheat anyone. What are you talking about?"

A sneer twisted his face. "Oh, come on, Colleen, you know what I'm talking about. The land. Your sheep walk. You knew I wanted it."

"Naturally, I knew that. Jonas told me."

"Yes, and that's where I made my mistake letting him in on the deal. Obviously he decided to marry you so the whole thing would be his."

Colleen's brows furrowed with total confusion. "What are you talking about, the whole thing?"

"It's simple, Colleen," he said with a smirk. "Your land is the prime spot for a ski resort. I've already got about a dozen backers willing to put up several million dollars."

"That's too bad," she gritted fiercely, "that you went to all that trouble, because I'd never let my mountain be turned into a playground for tourists!"

He laughed brashly. "And what do you think Jonas is going to do with it? Obviously he wanted it pretty badly to go so far as to marry you before I could get out here. Guess he stepped in and offered to pay your mortgages for you, didn't he?"

Colleen felt dizzy. "Why wouldn't he? He's my husband," she defended.

"Sure, Colleen," he voiced mockingly. "When are you going to wake up? You let one man take you for a sucker and now you've done it again."

"I'm not going to listen to this. You'd say anything to hurt me."

"It's not my fault if the truth hurts," he quipped. "I just tell it as I see it. And anyone with one good eye could see what's happened here. A sudden marriage. You were a woman alone, you needed money. Jonas provided it and along the way saw a way to help himself to something even bigger. After all, millions can't be compared to the few thousand he paid the bank for you."

"You're crazy, Roger! Jonas has no interest in a ski resort. He's going to keep my sheep, my land for me!"

He smiled smugly at the panicky rise in her voice. "I hope you have that in writing, Colleen. Otherwise, I think you've been one gullible woman."

"Jonas didn't know why you wanted that land. He told me so!"

"I figured you'd learned by now not to believe everything a man tells you. But as far as the land goes I'm going to see Jonas about it anyway. For the right amount he might be willing to sell it to me."

Colleen couldn't bear to hear anymore. She turned on her heel and quickly walked away. Her car was parked a block away just across from Jonas's law office. By the time Colleen reached it she was shaking uncontrollably. She slid inside and rested her forehead on the steering wheel as questions poured through her mind.

Could her cousin be telling the truth this time? Oh Lord, she didn't want to think so, but looking at it from an objective angle it seemed highly probable. The only reason Jonas had talked to her in the first place was because of the land. But that wasn't why he'd married her, her heart argued. He loved her, he'd told her so over and over. But then, so had Bradley, she thought sickly.

She lifted her head and was vaguely aware that tears were on her cheeks. Without thinking, she started the car and backed out of the parking space. She couldn't meet Jonas for lunch now. She didn't think she could bear to face him.

At the end of the block, she turned the car around and headed east. She drove in a stupor, automatically braking and accelerating through the traffic without being aware of what she was doing.

I hope you have that in writing. Roger's words played over and over in her mind as she recalled the evening she'd first talked to Jonas about the premarital agreement.

She'd still been doubting his motives for marrying her then and she'd wanted to make sure her land was safe. He'd agreed, she remembered, but he'd also made the excuse that he didn't have time to write one because of the trial. And by the time the case was over, he'd gotten Colleen into his bed and she'd melted like a piece of butter. Like a fool she'd believed it was for love, and she'd played right into his hands, telling him to forget the premarital agreement.

We're using each other, Colleen, she remembered him saying. *People do it all the time. You need money and I want to keep my land.* Damn him! And damn herself for ever believing him. He'd wanted to keep his land, all right, and hers along with it.

When the turnoff to the Slash D appeared on the horizon, Colleen pressed her foot down even harder on the gas pedal. She didn't want to go back there. Not now. Maybe never.

For the next fifteen miles she clung to the steering wheel, her movements wooden as she drove through the winding mountain road to her home.

The house was locked. She found the key under a flower pot by the steps and opened the front door. There was a musty, deserted smell about the place and her footsteps echoed hollowly as she walked through the house. The sound matched the emptiness in her heart.

Chapter Nine

Opal, has Colleen arrived yet?" Jonas asked his secretary over the office intercom. "She's fifteen minutes late."

"No, afraid not, Jonas. Would you like for me to call the ranch to make sure she's left? Something might have detained her."

"That's okay, Opal. I'll call myself." He released the button on the intercom and reached for the phone. Rose answered after the third ring.

"She left more than an hour ago, Jonas. Do you suppose she had car trouble?"

Jonas tapped his pen against the ink blotter on his desk. She was driving his Mercedes and it had always been very dependable. "I don't know, Rose. I'll have a look around town. She was thinking about buying a pair of riding boots. She's probably down at the western store and has forgotten the time. I'll call you later."

He put down the telephone, then left his desk and reached for his Stetson. He was tugging it down on his forehead when the intercom buzzed.

"Jonas, there's a man here who'd like to see you. He says he's an old friend. A Mr. Roger Boyd."

Jonas strode back to his desk to answer his secretary. "By all means, send him in, Opal," he said, his voice full of daggers. "He's just the man I want to see."

Jonas didn't bother taking off his hat or sitting down. Somehow he knew Roger was the reason Colleen still hadn't arrived, and he was going to get the immense pleasure of committing an assault and battery.

The door opened and Roger strode into the room. "Jonas, how are you, old boy?"

He stuck his hand out, but Jonas ignored it. "What are you doing here, Roger?"

"Now is that any way to greet an old friend?" he asked, frowning. Without an invitation he crossed the room, took a seat in a leather chair and made himself comfortable.

Jonas glared at him. "If you made a trip out here for Colleen's land, you can forget it. It's not for sale. Nor will it ever be."

"Well now, you say that like a man who's really sure of himself."

"I am."

Roger looked at him as if he expected Jonas to say more. When he didn't, Roger said, "You know, I knew you were a good lawyer. I just didn't realize how good until I ran into Colleen a few minutes ago."

Jonas was suddenly across the room and towering over him. "What have you been saying to my wife?"

The easy expression fell from Roger's face. "That you're a cheat, Jonas. You knew I wanted that land and you went to extreme measures to pull it out from under me."

In a blind fury Jonas reached down and grabbed the front of Roger's suit, jerking him to his feet. Then slowly he pulled the knot of Roger's tie until it tightened menacingly around the man's neck. "My wife's land is none of your business," he gritted. "My marriage is none of your business!"

Roger's eyes widened with fear as he stared up at Jonas's threatening face. "You married her to get that land! At least I would have paid her for it," he spluttered defensively.

Jonas wanted to kill him, but instead settled for a stiff right to Roger's jaw. The man staggered backward, then fell groaning across the leather chair.

"I married Colleen because I loved her," he said in a low, cutting voice. "Now, get the hell out of my office!"

After searching around town and not finding Colleen anywhere, Jonas decided to drive back to the ranch. On the way he used the car phone to call Rose, but she told him Colleen still hadn't shown up there.

Her disappearance frightened him. There was no telling what kind of lies Roger had put in her mind. Damn it! How could she have believed him?

Once at the Slash D, Jonas waited and watched for her, pacing restlessly from room to room. After an hour passed he decided she wasn't coming back, and he ran out the front door with Rose close on his heels.

"Jonas, she'll be back. You'll kill yourself driving too fast in that sports car!"

"I'm going to find her, Rose. I can't just sit around here waiting!"

Jonas roared down the drive with the housekeeper shaking her head after him.

Colleen sat on the flat rock, her knees drawn up to her chin, her hands linked at her ankles. Dangit lay beside her, his nose pressed against her hip.

After she'd changed clothes at her house, Colleen had driven out to the sheep camp and sent Virgil home.

At first the older man hadn't wanted to leave Colleen there alone, but she'd insisted, telling him to drive Jonas's Mercedes back to the ranch and leave her the Jeep.

The Jeep. She almost laughed when she thought of the old beat-up vehicle. It was probably the only thing she really owned besides Dangit.

Wistfully she stroked the dog's head as she looked out at the flock scattered along the mountainside. This had been her life for many years. The dog, the mountains, her sheep. It had been a lonely life, but at least living it hadn't hurt as she was hurting now.

She knew that sooner or later she would have to go back to the Slash D and face Jonas. Legally she was his wife, but legality didn't matter to her anymore. She'd given him her love, her trust. How could he have deceived her so?

Dangit suddenly lifted his head and growled. Colleen pulled herself out of her anguished reverie and looked down the mountain. Jonas was quickly climbing up toward her and for a moment she had the urge to run.

"Colleen, God Almighty, what are you doing up here?" he asked when he drew abreast of her.

Just the sight of him ripped at her heart. It was all she could do not to burst into tears. Her whole body was trembling as she spoke, "Sorry about our lunch date, Jonas."

He was in front of her, reaching down and taking hold of her shoulders. "Damn it, Colleen! I've been worried out of my mind. If I hadn't met Virgil on the road I wouldn't have had any idea where you were!"

God, he must be a good actor, she thought dazedly. The anxiety on his face looked so real she could almost believe it was.

She took a deep breath, looked away from him and at the sheep. "I was just sitting here thinking what a hell of a time I've had trying to hang on to all this. And I'm beginning to wonder why, or if anyone even cares."

Her voice was weary, almost rambling, and he wondered what kind of hell she'd been putting herself through. "I care, Colleen. I've cared from the very first, you know that."

His words brought her face back around to him. Anger tautened her lips and flashed in her green eyes. "Sure you did."

Jonas's fingers dipped into the flesh of her shoulders. "Colleen, I didn't come out here to talk around in circles! I know you saw Roger in town. What did he tell you?"

Unable to look at him, she closed her eyes tightly. "He told me lots of things. But on the whole, I guess you could say he told me why someone like you would marry someone like me."

Biting back a curse of frustration he said, "You know why I married you. I mean, at first I told you it was to save my ranch, but it wasn't. Not really. It took me a while to realize that, but—"

"Of course it wasn't to save your ranch!" she suddenly burst out, her eyes flying open. "You wanted my land for some damn ski resort! Well I'm telling you, Jonas, I'll fight you every step of the way on this! I don't care if you are a lawyer—"

Jonas shook her. "What are you talking about?" he asked in confusion. "What is this about a ski resort?"

"Don't play innocent with me!"

His face was set with fury. "Don't call me a liar!"

"You are!" she flung at him. "Roger said you knew about all of it, about the ski resort, the backers he'd already lined up to finance it, but you saw a chance to steal it from him by marrying me."

Jonas's brows rose with each word she spoke, until suddenly he was laughing. Colleen was so infuriated she wanted to slap him.

"Oh, Colleen," he said mockingly. "Surely you didn't believe that!"

Tears were on her face now. She was being ripped apart and he was being flip about it all. She'd never let another man touch her for as long as she lived!

"It's obvious. You made an excuse not to write that premarital agreement to give you more time."

"More time for what?" he asked innocently.

Her face flamed. "To—to physically persuade me to—forget it."

"Oh, hell, here! I'll write you one right now. These damn sheep can be the witnesses, or Dangit there. He looks intelligent enough."

Colleen stared inanely as he whipped his wallet out of his back pocket. He thumbed through it until he found a blank check.

"Don't worry," he told her, pulling out an ink pen and propping the piece of paper on his knee. "This will be perfectly legal. You can even watch over me while I have Opal notarize it."

He began to scrawl words quickly upon the back of the paper. As he did, something snapped inside of Colleen. "I—what are you writing on that?" she asked, her eyes on his hand as he wrote.

Jonas glanced up at her and Colleen could not mistake the hurt on his face. He made a disparaging grunt. "It says Colleen's land will always be Colleen's land. That she doesn't love her husband enough to trust him. And that she cares more about material things than she does me."

"That's not true!" she burst out, suddenly jumping to her feet.

His eyes narrowed with disgust as he stared back at her. "No? Well, it looks pretty obvious to me. You believed Roger over me. Ever since this whole thing started you've doubted me!"

"Surely you can understand why—"

"No! You haven't thought about me, period! My feelings never entered your thoughts. You were always too busy worrying about what I might try to steal from you."

His words cut deep, forcing her to turn away from him, or risk letting him see her tears. He was right. She'd made a horrible mess of everything. To love completely meant that you had to trust completely, too. She knew that now.

"You told me yourself that Roger would try to hurt you any way he could. Why did you believe him? Do I mean so little to you?"

She turned back to him and winced at the pain on his face. "I love you, Jonas. Even when I thought you only wanted my land, I couldn't help loving you." She looked back at him, blinking her eyes to ward off the stinging tears. "Maybe that's hard for you to believe. But I—for all these years I never believed in myself as a woman. I somehow thought that after Bradley no man would want me." Her eyes pleaded with him to understand. "Especially a man like you."

"I'm no different than any other man," he said, running a weary hand through his dark hair.

"In my eyes you're very different, Jonas," she said softly. "I guess that's because I love you so."

With a sigh, he lifted his face toward the sky. "I want to believe you, Colleen," he said huskily. "But how long will it be before you start to doubt me again?"

Colleen reached over and pulled the paper from his hand and crumpled it in her fist. "I'll never doubt you again, Jonas," she told him as he looked back down at her. "If you'll let me, I'll spend the rest of my life proving it to you."

The guarded look in his eyes melted away and with a groan, he reached out and hauled her into his arms. "I'm going to make sure you do," he said against her hair. "I love you, Colleen, and I don't intend to let you leave me again."

Her arms came around his waist and she pressed herself close to him. Just being in his arms made her happy, and she realized that this man had become her life. The land and the sheep no longer mattered. She just wanted to know she would always have his love. "Wherever you are is where I want to be," she whispered as tears of happiness began to roll down her cheeks.

Jonas took her face between his palms and kissed her gently. Colleen's lips clung to his, silently pledging her love.

"Let's go home," he murmured once the kiss ended.

Colleen nodded up at him, her eyes glistening with love and happiness. "Yes, let's go home."

Jonas took her hand and began to lead her back down the mountainside. In her other hand was the crumpled piece of paper. As they walked, Colleen relaxed her fingers and allowed it to fall to the ground behind them and blow away with the wind.

* * * * *

PASSPORT TO ROMANCE VACATION SWEEPSTAKES

OFFICIAL RULES

SWEEPSTAKES RULES AND REGULATIONS. NO PURCHASE NECESSARY.

HOW TO ENTER:

1. To enter, complete this official entry form and return with your invoice in the envelope provided, or print your name, address, telephone number and age on a plain piece of paper and mail to: Passport to Romance, P.O. Box #1397, Buffalo, N.Y. 14269-1397. No mechanically reproduced entries accepted.
2. All entries must be received by the Contest Closing Date, midnight, December 31, 1990 to be eligible.
3. Prizes: There will be ten (10) Grand Prizes awarded, each consisting of a choice of a trip for two people to: i) London, England (approximate retail value $5,050 U.S.); ii) England, Wales and Scotland (approximate retail value $6,400 U.S.); iii) Caribbean Cruise (approximate retail value $7,300 U.S.); iv) Hawaii (approximate retail value $ 9,550 U.S.); v) Greek Island Cruise in the Mediterranean (approximate retail value $12,250 U.S.); vi) France (approximate retail value $7,300 U.S.).
4. Any winner may choose to receive any trip or a cash alternative prize of $5,000.00 U.S. in lieu of the trip.
5. Odds of winning depend on number of entries received.
6. A random draw will be made by Nielsen Promotion Services, an independent judging organization on January 29, 1991, in Buffalo, N.Y., at 11:30 a.m. from all eligible entries received on or before the Contest Closing Date. Any Canadian entrants who are selected must correctly answer a time-limited, mathematical skill-testing question in order to win. Quebec residents may submit any litigation respecting the conduct and awarding of a prize in this contest to the Régie des loteries et courses du Quebec.
7. Full contest rules may be obtained by sending a stamped, self-addressed envelope to: "Passport to Romance Rules Request", P.O. Box 9998, Saint John, New Brunswick, E2L 4N4.
8. Payment of taxes other than air and hotel taxes is the sole responsibility of the winner.
9. Void where prohibited by law.

PASSPORT TO ROMANCE VACATION SWEEPSTAKES

OFFICIAL RULES

SWEEPSTAKES RULES AND REGULATIONS. NO PURCHASE NECESSARY.

HOW TO ENTER:

1. To enter, complete this official entry form and return with your invoice in the envelope provided, or print your name, address, telephone number and age on a plain piece of paper and mail to: Passport to Romance, P.O. Box #1397, Buffalo, N.Y. 14269-1397. No mechanically reproduced entries accepted.
2. All entries must be received by the Contest Closing Date, midnight, December 31, 1990 to be eligible.
3. Prizes: There will be ten (10) Grand Prizes awarded, each consisting of a choice of a trip for two people to: i) London, England (approximate retail value $5,050 U.S.); ii) England, Wales and Scotland (approximate retail value $6,400 U.S.); iii) Caribbean Cruise (approximate retail value $7,300 U.S.); iv) Hawaii (approximate retail value $ 9,550 U.S.); v) Greek Island Cruise in the Mediterranean (approximate retail value $12,250 U.S.); vi) France (approximate retail value $7,300 U.S.).
4. Any winner may choose to receive any trip or a cash alternative prize of $5,000.00 U.S. in lieu of the trip.
5. Odds of winning depend on number of entries received.
6. A random draw will be made by Nielsen Promotion Services, an independent judging organization on January 29, 1991, in Buffalo, N.Y., at 11:30 a.m. from all eligible entries received on or before the Contest Closing Date. Any Canadian entrants who are selected must correctly answer a time-limited, mathematical skill-testing question in order to win. Quebec residents may submit any litigation respecting the conduct and awarding of a prize in this contest to the Régie des loteries et courses du Quebec.
7. Full contest rules may be obtained by sending a stamped, self-addressed envelope to: "Passport to Romance Rules Request", P.O. Box 9998, Saint John, New Brunswick, E2L 4N4.
8. Payment of taxes other than air and hotel taxes is the sole responsibility of the winner.
9. Void where prohibited by law.

 RLS-DIR

VACATION SWEEPSTAKES

MONTH 2 ENTRY

Official Entry Form

Yes, enter me in the drawing for one of ten Vacations-for-Two! If I'm a winner, I'll get my choice of any of the six different destinations being offered — and I won't have to decide until after I'm notified!

Return entries with invoice in envelope provided along with Daily Travel Allowance Voucher. Each book in your shipment has two entry forms — and the more you enter, the better your chance of winning!

Name ____________________

Address ____________________ Apt.

City ____________ State/Prov. ____________ Zip/Postal Code

Daytime phone number ____________________
Area Code

☐ I am enclosing a Daily Travel Allowance Voucher in the amount of $__________ Write in amount revealed beneath scratch-off

PASSPORT WIN 1 of 10 Vacations SEE INSIDE TO ROMANCE

VACATION SWEEPSTAKES

MONTH 2 ENTRY

Official Entry Form

Yes, enter me in the drawing for one of ten Vacations-for-Two! If I'm a winner, I'll get my choice of any of the six different destinations being offered — and I won't have to decide until after I'm notified!

Return entries with invoice in envelope provided along with Daily Travel Allowance Voucher. Each book in your shipment has two entry forms — and the more you enter, the better your chance of winning!

Name ____________________

Address ____________________ Apt.

City ____________ State/Prov. ____________ Zip/Postal Code

Daytime phone number ____________________
Area Code

☐ I am enclosing a Daily Travel Allowance Voucher in the amount of $__________ Write in amount revealed beneath scratch-off

CPS-TWO